Write To Woof 2016

*Edited by
Diana Kathryn
Plopa*

Grey Wolfe Publishing, LLC
PO Box 1088
Birmingham, Michigan 48009
www.GreyWolfePublishing.com

© 2016 Grey Wolfe Publishing, LLC
Published by Grey Wolfe Publishing, LLC
www.GreyWolfePublishing.com
All Rights Reserved

ISBN: 978-1628281347
Library of Congress Control Number: 2016940438

Write To Woof 2016

Edited by
Diana Kathryn Plopa

Dedication

Write To Woof is an annual anthology published by Grey Wolfe Publishing. The goal of this year's collection is to bring awareness to the roles dogs play in our lives... as companions, helpers and teachers. Whether pure-bred or rescued Mutt; each enhances our lives like no other creature on earth.

This book is lovingly dedicated to Bear. His photo appears on the Contributing Author Page. He was a tremendous companion and teacher to our family. We miss him dearly.

Acknowledgements

We would like to send out a special *Thank You* to the authors who submitted their work for this book. It is because of your dedication to dogs, as well as the writing craft, that we have been able to produce such a spectacular tribute to our furry friends!

We also want to thank the good people of *Detroit Dog Rescue* who work tirelessly day after day to make sure that abandoned dogs from the inner city streets of Detroit are well cared for and connected with life-long, loving homes.

And finally, we want to thank *you*, the person who purchased this book and are about to read it. Because of your interest in dogs, or perhaps because of the relationship you have with one of the authors, dogs with particular challenges will be partnered with extraordinary families as they grow to trust again... feel safe again... love again... forever.

Contents

1. A Poem About A Four-Legged Friend   Norbert Gora
2. A Poetic Tribute to Sammy The   Mark Hudson
    Christmas Dog
3. One More Dead Dog Story   Diane Payne
4. Billy's New Friend   Theresa Nielsen
5. Both Bit By Barney   Mark Hudson
6. Buck   Mark Hudson
7. Chibi 1 & 2   Joann Grisetti
8. Cindy   Carol Hanson
9. Damn Dog Died   Edward Ahern
10. Cooper's Trick   Pamela Murry
11. Dog Days of Autumn   Sharon Frame Gay
12. DoG: Man's Best Friend   Thomas K. Tabor
13. Dog   Renata Rzepecki-
                                          Dawidowicz
14. Doggedly Downtrodden   A.J. Huffman
15. For I will Consider My Dog Chico   Betty Hartnett
16. Found In Translation   Jon Moray
17. From Chico   Betty Hartnett
18. From Willow To Nome   John C. Mannone
19. Gunshot   Briana J. Weiss
20. Hound Sounds   Terry Sanville
21. In Memory of My Uncle's Dogs   Mark Hudson
22. January 14th   Jay Dardes
23. Lucy   Lisa M. Scuderi-
                                          Burkimisher
24. My Canine Comforter   A.J. Huffman
25. My Canine Friend   Celia P. Ransom

26.	My Chihuahua Tries	A.J. Huffman
27.	My Literary Lions	Patricia Holland
28.	Of Demons and Dogs	John C. Mannone
29.	Of Possums and Poetry	Stephanie Madan
30.	Porch Guardian	Christopher Woods
31.	Squirrel Spaniel (Cinquain)	Irish Goat
32.	Strolling in the Park	Renee Babtenjany
33.	Thanksgiving with the Dogs!	Mark Hudson
34.	The Anchor	Matt McGee
35.	The Joy of Walking	Betty Hartnet
36.	The Leash	Lynne Adams
37.	A Story of Hope: Just an Old Farm Dog	Patricia Holland
38.	The Pack (Nonet, Progressive, Reverse)	Irish Goat
39.	Warmth (Sedoka, Triple)	Irish Goat
40.	Where's The Beef?	Stephanie Madan
41.	Woodford's Big Game	Patricia Holland
42.	You Mean More than the Vastness of the Sky	Norbert Gora
43.	You Prefer People	Betty Hartnett

Contributing Authors

The Grey Wolfe Pack

Detroit Dog Rescue

St. Claire Shores, MI

1.
A Poem About A Four-Legged Friend
Norbert Gora

When you're with me
shawl woven with happiness
wraps my body, soothes the soul.

You look attentively at me,
reading from my face every emotion
as if I were an open book.

I would like to know
what is behind the wisdom of your eyes,
in the depths of your heart,
so important for me.

What drives this excitement
when you start competing
with the wind.

What do you feel
when you commune
with the richness of the world
of sounds, inaudible to humans.

Whose scents
brings the blowing wind,
stroking leaves on tall trees.

Clouds composed of my questions
swirl above our heads,
but I believe that will come
rain of answers.

Two hearts, though so different,
connects them a thread
as strong as strings of angelic harps.

2.
A Poetic Tribute to Sammy The Christmas Dog
Mark Hudson

Inspired by the article, Sammy the Christmas Dog, by David Witter from New City Magazine, Volume 30, no. 339.

A young Chicago couple moved to Portage Park,
and found a nice dog that did more than just bark.
Around Christmas '98', on a cold, snowy day,
they found a tiny shoebox that contained a stray.
A holiday box with a red ribbon around it;
the puppy inside had them glad they found it.
Someone could no longer keep their puppy,
so they left it at the doorstep of some yuppies.
They named him Sammy, Sammy Sosa the hero,
saving the puppy from weather below zero.
At a Christmas party, Sammy discovered,
some pot which he ate, but then he recovered.
He ate some marijuana, about a quarter ounce,
and onto an Italian beef sandwich he pounced.
Fortunately, they took him to an emergency room,
where they saved his life from the stuff he consumed.
In 2009, Sammy swam the Chicago River,
the rainfall made rapids, yet Sammy didn't shiver.
In late November, they found cancer in his heart,
the Christmas dog was preparing to depart.
The sad couple felt Christmas was a letdown,
knowing that Sammy would no longer be around.
The Christmas dog died in February 2010,
God rest Sammy, and you merry gentlemen, (and women.)

3.
One More Dead Dog Story
Diane Payne

Recently, my older dog became deathly ill. It was Labor Day weekend, which meant the closest vet was one hundred miles away since we don't have any vets on call for after-hour emergencies in my area. After leaving Max at the hospital, uncertain if I'd ever see him again, I came home to walk my other dog. The two dogs always walked on a coupler, and Logan didn't want to leave the house without Max. I had to coax him outside. He'd stop on the street, turn back to look at the house, and refuse to move. I was crying, dreading seeing any neighbors. Logan was enduring his own form of despair.

It wasn't long, and I ran into a neighbor walking her dog. As soon as she asked, "Where's Max?" I burst into tears, apologized for crying, and rambled on about how his sudden illness and current hospitalization. This isn't the first time I've walked these same streets weeping while a pet was near death in the hospital. People probably think I'd be more stoic by now.

The blood work showed that Max's liver and kidneys were shutting down. I called my daughter Ania, who is a grad student in another state, warning her that Max may by dying. "Keep him alive," she sobbed.

When I first arrived at the hospital, they put Max on oxygen and asked if I wanted to keep him on life support until he could see a vet. "We need to warn you that costs $500 for each half hour we keep him alive." I drove this far to see a vet, so I agreed to pay. After I broke down crying, they ushered me into a private room to spare the other people in the waiting room any more anguish, since all of our pets had to be quite ill to be at the emergency after-hour hospital.

At one point, the vet returned to say Max was breathing on his own.   A sign of hope.   He suggested that Max had been ill for a while, and I may not have noticed.   "Animals like to hide their illness," he said.

Guilt.

I kept replaying the week, wondering what symptoms I may have missed.   Max was at the lake, walking back and forth in the shallow water, like a senior citizen doing aerobics at a pool.   This was bliss, not a dog suffering from a lingering illness.   The day before he became ill, we took three walks in the misty rain, relieved to have a break from the Arkansas heat.

Eight years ago, I drove Max to this same hospital in the middle of the night when he was in status mode.   Seizure after seizure after seizure.   The vets kept calling me throughout the night, wanting permission to put him down.   I was adamant that he wanted to live and told them that unless he was suffering, not them, I wanted Max to remain in the induced coma and kept alive because I believed he would live.   "He has a less than one percent chance of living."

Stubborn, I banked on that fraction of a percent.

He did live and never had another seizure.

There were no percentages being discussed this time.

Early the next morning, Max had to be removed from the emergency hospital to a regular vet, but they didn't think I should bring him to our hometown vet because he was vomiting and could dehydrate in the long car ride.   They moved Max to the day clinic across the street from the hospital.   This vet wanted to do x-rays, more tests, and kept repeating, "Max is a very sick dog."

When Max was home, the minute I'd start to put my shoes on, Logan would jump all over Max, eager for the walk.   Now I had to go to Logan on the couch and coax him out the door. Once again, Logan stood in the road, refusing to move. I don't know if he felt he was not being loyal to Max by taking a walk without him, or if he just didn't see any point in taking a walk without Max. There are so many things I'll never understand about how animals feel about life. Or death. I coaxed Logan out the door and walked down the street, sobbing, hoping I wouldn't run into any neighbors. I had believed I'd be driving to Little Rock early in the morning and bringing Max home, not walking Logan alone while Max remained hospitalized one hundred miles from home.

In the beginning, eleven years ago, Ania and I each carried a cat in a doggy pack, and rollerbladed around a pond at her school, while another dog, Barto, ran behind us. Having lived in Arizona before moving to Arkansas, I thought I saw a javelina, which didn't make sense but I felt compelled to check it out, near the baseball field, and tromped in the dirt to explore. There was Max running back to his littermates who were burrowed in the ground. We pulled Max and the rest of the litter from their hiding place, put the pups in the car with the rest of our critters, found homes for the other pups, but kept Max. There was something about Max that made me feel immediately connected to him.

Even though Max was already bigger than the cats, Ania wanted me to walk Barto on the leash while she carried Max in a doggy pack, the pack that was always intended for cats, not dogs.

Walking Logan, I thought about was how Ania may never see Max again.

Later that day, a vet who knew Max and had an office fifty miles from our home, called the other vet so they could have an honest vet-to-vet talk. They decided Max could be transported, and he would have the same chance of survival with him, and did not need to spend another night at the emergency hospital. Convinced that this vet could take care of Max, I returned to Little Rock to retrieve Max. When we were loading Max into my car, Max gave me such a hopeful look as I placed him on his doggy bed, certain he was going home, and this hellish experience was finally over. The vet assistant who had also worked at the emergency hospital said, "I've seen another dog like this. Didn't you say you walked him this weekend? Maybe he's suffering from heat stroke. It happens."

More guilt.

When I left Max with this other vet, he placed him in the kennel with an IV. "I'm adding glucose. This should perk him up." Max tried to get up, hoping to come home with me. "That's a good sign," he said. I told Max I'd be back to visit him the next morning. Except he died in the morning, and my last image is of Max giving me that hopeful look he'd be going home with me. That image haunts me today. Maybe I should have just let him die at home in my arms?

Even more guilt.

I had to decide if I was going to pick up Max and bury him at home or have him cremated, but I wasn't ready to make the decision when I answered the death phone call from the vet. I believed that Max was going to live. I called Ania, and she suggested that I have him cremated. She probably believed cremating would be easier on me since the two of us have held our pets while they died at home, then we've dug their holes to bury them, howling with grief.

A neighbor friend offered to bring Max home. This was such an incredible act of kindness. She called her husband to say I was digging Max's grave, and he left his job to help me. I'm forever grateful for their compassion.

I wanted the other animals to have a chance to see Max one more time, to come out to the yard to say their goodbyes. All of us needed closure. The pets came outside, smelled Max, then ran back inside the house.   Dead Max was unbearable for everyone.

This summer, while visiting an old friend, we were walking her dog, and she told me the hardest part of when her other dog had died was walking just one dog.   She deliberately took other routes to avoid neighbors.

A week after Max died, the young neighbor girl came up to the door, a bit afraid to ask if she could walk Logan with me, thinking things may have changed now that Max had died.   These kids liked to walk the dogs with me after they came home from school.   Her younger brother usually walked Max since he was a bit smaller than Logan.   Now, the younger brother stands in the yard and watches his sister and I walk Logan, unsure how he fits into the scheme of things since there is only one dog to walk. On our first walk together without Max, she kept bringing up Max stories.   Our favorite dog-walking stories involve Max's poop.   He saved his poops for his daily walks and loved all the attention he got while the kids squealed with perverse delight, watching me pick up his steamy poops.   "It's a freshly baked Tootsie Roll.   Want one?" I'd ask, offering the bag of poop to the kids. Who wouldn't enjoy these great walks talking about Max's poop and Logan's farts?

Even though it has been one month almost to the day since Max has died, twice last week people yelled from their homes as Logan and I were out walking, "Hey, where's the black dog? I haven't seen him in weeks." Do they really expect me to yell back: "Max died!" For some reason, I thought I'd finally be free of the dead dog questions.   The first two weeks were non-stop questions, and then endless sad stories of their dead pets. I dreaded every walk.   Maybe Logan was trying to tell me something by not wanting to leave the house.

Logan and I will be out walking, and I will hear a car slow down. I brace myself for another neighbor who is about to pull over and ask what happened to the black dog. When I say that Max is dead, they say, "That's what I figured. He was old, right?" Then they go on and tell me about all the dogs they've buried in their yards, and I hope another car will come down the street so they'll have to move on before I need to endure any more dead dog stories.

One neighbor stopped to tell me how her parents just put down their old cat. But unlike me, who spent my first two paychecks of the school year on vet bills, her dad just killed the cat. "Cheaper that way," she said as I hurried off not wanting to know the graphic details.

After these walks, I've gone home and looked up the weather of the day I last walked Max. 70's and rainy. But the humidity. The damn humidity. I've researched causes for liver and kidney failure. Endless possibilities.

I don't blame all those vets for not knowing what caused Max to die, but I do wish no one had assumed it could have been because of our last walk or because I somehow didn't notice that he had been sick for a long while.

I've buried many pets, so this grief isn't unfamiliar. It's not that death makes me more vulnerable or immortal. It's that while I'm immersed in grief over losing a dear pet, that immersion of grief blends in with all the other losses of life, and for a while, I just need to be immobilized in this profound sadness.

When I'm in the yard, I notice the flowers the neighbor kids have dropped over the fence onto Max's grave. One day I noticed a seashell with the words painted: Max was a great dog.

Max was a great dog. The kids get it.

4.
Billy's New Friend
Theresa Nielsen

The day started out like any other, sunny and warm. Still, I was nervous; it was my first day of a new job. At my age, it isn't easy. Being a caregiver is rewarding, meeting new people is a challenge. There are always high expectations, measuring up to others."

I did my best to put that behind me and rang the doorbell.

"Hi, Mrs. Harris, I'm Jessie Bryant."

"Yes, of course, come in. Billy is in his room."

"You have a lovely home," I said. I noticed right away the photos on the walls and the colorful blue quilt on the sofa.

"Let's go up to his room, shall we." I followed her up the steps and down a long hallway.

"Billy, she called out, its Mom. Can you open the door?"

"No Mom, can't do it." came the voice on the other side.

Mrs. Harris looked at me. "I knew he would do this, he's shy. But you'll get used to him, I'm sure."

"Yes, I will."

"Can you tell me a little more about him, what he likes perhaps?"

"Sure, how about a cup of tea while we chat," she said as we women went back downstairs.

"Billy has a lot of fears, some are normal because he doesn't see well. He is afraid of water, loud noises. When we are out in the community, he is afraid of big trucks, horns honking. And dogs, I'm not sure why the dogs, we have never owned a dog."

"Perhaps he heard one barking loudly at some point, lots of people are afraid of dogs."

"He's always been so happy though. Anyway, you're here now," she said pouring the water into the tea cups. "Curiosity usually gets the best of him and he'll come down on his own. I'm sure you have a lot of experience with kids like Billy."

"I do, and I enjoy working with all of them, and getting to know them."

"Mom, I'm down here, said Billy. I'm here."

I put her tea cup down when I heard his voice. Billy was tall, long legged with a cheerful smile and curly blond hair. His eyes were green, staring straight at me.

"Billy, I would like you to meet Jessie."

"Who Mom, who is it," he said putting his hands out towards her.

Mom placed his hands in Jessie's. "She is going to be helping out around here, spending time with you."

"Hi Billy, it's nice to meet you."

"Me too, "he said. *He has a deep voice for a young man.*

"Are you going to take me home with you," he asked.

"No, but I will visit often. Is that okay with you?"

Without warning, he hugged me. His grip was firm. Mom gently pulled him away.

"Billy likes hugs, singing, most foods and jokes," said Mom.

"Well, I'm happy to get started with him. I will see you both tomorrow."

*****

That night, after dinner I sat down and read over Billy's notes from the agency. He liked stuffed animals, fuzzy toys and ice cream. He was an only child; he had just recently turned twelve years old. He had some developmental disabilities; his mom home schooled him and his Dad was away from home a lot, traveling for his job.

*****

The next morning I packed my bag with goodies. I decided on my favorite blue shorts, a grey t-shirt and comfortable shoes. It would be a long day. I took Skippy for his walk and headed out for my first day.

Billy greeted me at the door.

"Hi Jessie, it's you. He gave me a hug. Are you ready?" he wanted to know.

"I am. Today we are going to hang around here and get to know each other."

Billy smiled.

"So what would you like to do today," I asked.

"Eat ice cream, play. Will you play, Jessie?"

"Sure I will, let's go outside."

Mom stood behind him smiling. "He didn't stay shy long, did he."

"No, this is great."

Together the two of us went out the back door into the yard. It was all fenced in, there were bird feeders in the trees, a tire swing and a large sandbox fit for a king. In the corner of the yard there was a picnic table with an umbrella.

"Billy, can we sit down here for a bit," I asked. I took out her notebook and several different color crayons. I saw Billy watching me. "Billy, my favorite color is blue, and I like the sky. Do you have a favorite color?" I asked.

"I like black, and I like dirt."

"Why do you like dirt?" I asked.

"Because I can imagine it to be whatever I want."

"What do you want it to be today?"

"Just dirt, so we can play in it. Do you want to play in the dirt with me?" he wanted to know.

"Of course we can."

Billy and I played in the dirt for a long while, until it was time to wash up for lunch. After lunch we sat on the porch swing. Billy munched on an apple while I read him stories.

It was time to go home, and I was ready for a bath. Billy was too.

*****

When I visited again three days later, he ran out the door to greet me. "I missed you Jessie, I'm glad to see you."

"It's good to see you too, what should we do today?"

"Can we play in the dirt again; I want to build a castle, a big castle."

"Great, I like castles," I said

I talked with mom for a minute until Billy pulled on my blouse, he wanted to go outside.

"See you later Billy," said Mom but he was already out the door.

Billy got in the sandbox and pushed all the sand into a big pile in the center. There were different shapes and sizes of toys to use for building a castle. I watched his hands, so busy filling the shapes and setting them on the edge. I was lost in thought for a moment.

"Jessie, aren't you going to help me?" he asked.

"Oh yes, here I am. Do you mind if my little dog joins us, he isn't real."

"Okay, he said. What color is he?"

"He's brown, black and a little white." I put the dog on a blanket near where me and Billy were playing. "You can pet him if you want."

"Maybe not," he said.

Soon we had built a whole town of sandcastles, big and small. I could tell Billy had done this many times before. When I looked up from digging, I saw Mom standing in the door, watching us.

"Billy how does the dirt feel in your hands?" I asked.

"Neat, like pebbles at the beach. Or a warm blanket."

"That is how my dog feels, like a warm blanket. I have a real dog at home."

"Does he sleep with you Jessie?"

"Yes, he does at the foot of the bed."

"Are you afraid of him, like if he sat on you?"

"No, not at all. He is small and really sweet, he just curls up to sleep after his cookie," I explained.

"He has a cookie?" asked Billy.

"Yes, every night, just a little one."

I noticed then that Billy was touching the dog, moving his fingers through the fur.

"Jessie, he asked, do you think your dog would let me pet him?"

"I'm sure he wouldn't mind. You could give him a treat."

"Can I meet him soon?"

"Sure, after I talk to your mom. She might like to meet him too."

"Jessie, I like you."

It had been three weeks since I had met Billy. my heart fluttered, tears fell against my face.

Mom agreed it was fine to meet the dog. This was going to be a big step for Billy.

*****

The next day, I gathered Skippy's leash, a handful of treats and a toy. "C'mon Skippy, we have work to do."

Billy was waiting at the door when I arrived, dancing on one foot and then the other. "Hi Jessie, ils this him?" he said holding out his hands.

"This is Skippy, let's go inside where I can put him down."

"Hi Mom," I said when we entered the room. "How are you?"

"Good, dogs are all he has talked about since you left."

"I'm glad to hear it; I think it will be a good experience for him."

Billy sat on the floor next to me, Skippy sniffed his shoes, his pants and licked his hands. "Does he like me Jessie, does he?" asked Billy, excited.

"I think Skippy has made a new friend, don't you Mom?"

I put Billy's hands on Skippy's back, "What do you think of his fur."

"It tickles me, it's fuzzy," he said laughing.

"Do you like him?" I asked.

"I do, I do."

Mom was crying, Billy didn't notice. He was hugging Skippy.

"I love you, Skippy," he said.

I looked up at Mom again.

She whispered, "Thank you."

5.
Both Bit By Barney
Mark Hudson

On a summer vacation we're driving through Wisconsin,
my niece Ashley had a stuffed goat from Al Johnson's.
We're all reminiscing about childhoods long ago,
my sister discusses neighbors we used to know.
Her neighbor had a dog Barney, who bit her,
the dog was put to sleep which made her quite bitter.
My dad said, "I was bit by a dog named Barney, too,
I told the owners to see what they could do.
They gave me a dollar to get some ice cream,
I forgot about the bite and fell for their scheme."
Bit by two Barneys, father and daughter,
we stopped at a lighthouse, and went by some water.

6.
Buck
Mark Hudson

*A poem inspired by reading Jack London's all-time classic
dog story, "A Call of the Wild,"*

Buck lived in sun-kissed Santa Clara,
the sunshine's rays shone like mascara.
Judge Miller was the owner of the verandas,
where he made his living through Miranda's.
The judge's daughters, Mollie and Alice,
played with Buck in a home like a palace.
But because of a gardener named Manuel,
Buck was sold into a form of doggerel.
He was kidnapped to be bought and sold,
in the gigantic westward rush for gold.
They put Buck in a big brass collar,
in order to make a ton of dollars.
The kidnappers had hidden motives,
they transferred Buck to locomotives.
What happened to Buck wasn't his fault,
he was sold to a man named Perrault.
And so the sledding expedition kept going,
it was fifty below zero and snowing.
The first dog couldn't go on and got weak,
and so the men shot him, showing blood can leak.
All the dogs in the pack could just tell,
that that could be there fate as well.
One by one, the dogs began to drop,
But Buck was the one who didn't stop.
Based on a real dog that Jack London knew,
The book was a classic, on people it grew.
It shows that a dog can be a hero in a story,

even if the g-rated violence is still gory.
So can anyone outdo London's "Call of the Wild?"
The library of congress has no new things filed.
And literature changes, human nature does not,
and dogs remain loyal, weather warm, cold, or hot.

7.
CHIBI 1 & 2
Joann Grisetti

Neighbors told my parents they should buy a dog to decrease the possibility of robbery. We found a little puppy and named her Chibi. She was a light brown mutt, very sweet and friendly with us. I loved to brush her, walk her, and play with her after school. Full of energy as she bounced around the house, Chibi exhibited the same fidgety tendencies I did. Although more successful on my own, Chibi loved to hunt butterflies with me in the vacant lot. Curiosity led her to explore her world as I did, as far as she could go.

sniffing dusty streets
completes her business quickly
the thunder rumbles

We let her out mornings into the vacant lot next door once she was housebroken. One morning when I called her to come back inside, she did not respond in her normal fashion. I thought, she must be playing a game with me. I called her again after eating breakfast, anger building when she did not come. I had to go to school, where was she? We found her across the street under a parked car. The neighbors put out rat poison, and Chibi had wandered over, intrigued by a strange smell.

distant rays of light
popping suddenly through trees
whose dog is barking?

Offered a second dog from the same breeder; we named her Chibi as well. A sweet dog, soon housebroken; we never let her out alone, though. She barked at anyone who came onto the porch, but not at those who stayed in the street. Smart enough to know where her property ended, she endeared herself to my family.

After a year, we moved into an apartment building and thought it best for Chibi not to be confined. We gave her to Ikukosan (the maid) to raise. They both found pleasure in the new arrangement, although it took a week or so for the adjustment. I visited Chibi at Ikukosan's house throughout the next two years.

bookbinding bent
from many readings
the dog asleep

8.
CINDY
Carol Hanson

When I was seven years old, I met my best friend Cindy. I somehow knew on that spring day that we were going to bond, and that I would be able to trust her with my deepest thoughts and secrets for eternity or until we both got really old.

The aging clapboard farmhouse where I met Cindy was only a block south of my home, but a world of difference from the brick or aluminum sided ranches of our neighborhood. Many were purchased on the G.I. Bill, including our own. Where Cindy lived was a completely different way of life, as it was zoned farmland.

First of all, the family living there had eleven children. Having two digits in the number made it seem gargantuan! At the Jackson's farm, there was also a chicken coop, a horse, and a dog that just had a litter of puppies a few weeks before. Something was always giving birth at that house it seemed!

My brother Ken and I both had friends at the Jackson's that were our ages. It was kind of hard not to find someone your own age there! One day Mrs. Jackson, who could have a gruff way about her, asked if we would like one of the puppies. Like was not a strong enough word! How about love?!!!

We raced home to ask our mom. We knew this had to be a face-to-face conversation. I told my mom that the dog was a female Pekinese, and just the cutest thing ever. I don't even remember if she called my dad at work for his input or not. I just know the resounding answer was yes!

We brought the dog home, and my mom inquired as to whether we were sure it was a Pekinese. We had somehow forgotten to mention that it was also part Beagle! No matter, my mom loved her and named her Cindy. Cindy, I thought to myself, was a way prettier name than the one I got stuck with. I let that thought pass like a wispy cloud on a warm summer day.

Cindy became the mascot of the neighborhood. She was special and smart beyond words. Everyone liked that she could "sit pretty" as we called it. In other words, she could sit up on her hind legs, like a circus animal. Since we lived on a corner lot, Cindy was able to take in things from a lot of different perspectives. For instance, the sound of the ice cream truck got her attention. She knew that even if we didn't buy ice cream every time, the ice cream man would still stop and give her pieces of broken cones if he had them.

Also in the summer, we would take her to Play School on the day of the Annual Dog Parade. Play School was a summer program at our elementary school that had all kinds of fun things to do, and no school work. We dressed Cindy up in some of my old clothes, and would embellish them by adding ribbons, sequins, and lace. Anything we had laying around that wasn't being used. My mom even embroidered her name on a hat. The moms would all come out and cheer and my mom would throw Dog Yummies to everyone's pet at the end. It was a fun day, for sure.

On Saturday's, Cindy would curl up beside me to watch *Fury* and *My Friend Flicka* on TV. I often wondered if she could still remember the horse that had been at her first house. These shows just seemed to hold her attention.

Although Cindy was a house dog, my dad built her a doghouse. There was a stake in the ground, and a good length of chain we would attach to her collar. One day when I was in 4th grade, Cindy pulled the stake out of the ground, and somehow ended up at my school with the chain and stake still attached. It was *clank clank clanking* along the sidewalk, making all kinds of racket. I was glad we were at recess when she was spotted. I was so afraid that the dog catcher would pick her up. We feared the dog catcher like nothing else. The sight of that white truck with bars on the windows was enough to raise the hackles on every dog around.

Cindy was enjoying her newfound freedom, and I couldn't get her to come to me. Several kids were trying to circle her to no avail. I was so scared, I thought I was going to cry. Luckily, it had been Hotdog Day at our school, and Mr. Brandon our janitor, came out with a hotdog and that finally got Cindy's attention. He gave me the hotdog and he retreated to the end of the rope and the stake. Cindy wolfed down that hotdog, and then gave me some much needed kisses.

I called my mom so she wouldn't worry that Cindy was on the loose. Mrs. Hubble, the principal, gave me, and my best human friend Debby, permission to take Cindy home. I was so glad to be a walker on that day than ever before. Cindy had finally calmed down. I told her "No Dog Yummies today." The hot dog had been her treat.

Cindy also helped me out at the dire dismal dinner table. I was a very picky eater, and there were two things that I hated more than anything. The first was mashed potatoes. Just the sound of that *thwack* as those potatoes came in for a landing on those pink Melmac dishes, still makes me cringe. The other food I detested was roast "beast." Cindy knew where the goodies were going to land, and she placed herself next to me like a favorite book on a shelf. She rescued me many a time, and I had to thank her that I had made it to dessert. Phew!!! It seemed the time between dinner and dessert was as long as the Mississippi River.

I was lucky enough to grow up with Cindy all through school and college. When I took a job in Pittsburgh, I said *"Get along home Cindy, Cindy."* That had always been our catch phrase, from an old song I heard on the radio. Three months later my parents came to see me and to check out my new apartment. I knew they wouldn't be bringing Cindy, because I only had a one bedroom, and they would be staying at a motel. I asked who was watching Cindy, and my mom told me God was watching her, and that she was in dog heaven now. I knew that Cindy's health had deteriorated before I left, but she had lived to give our family sixteen wonderful years. My parents took Cindy to a dog cemetery in Taylor for burial, so I knew Cindy would always be close in distance and in heart. For one last time I thought "Get along home Cindy, Cindy."

9.
Cooper's Trick
Pamela Murry

Gus heard his name as he stepped into the apartment and stopped in his tracks. Rather than let the door slam in his usual careless way, he gently pushed the heavy door into the latch and stood in the genkan, listening.

"Bonnie, we've been over this so many times. Keeping a dog in Tokyo is a really bad idea. We'll wait till we're back in Michigan. Then you can get any dog you want," said Dad.

"He's already eleven. If we stay in Japan another six years, Gus will grow up without a dog—not to mention Jackie," said Mom, referring to Gus's older sister.

"Well, it won't be six more years, you know that. Things can change at any time," Dad said.

Gus sighed. Perching on the low bench next to the shoe closet, he set his baseball glove and ball on the tile floor while he untied his shoelaces. More than anything else in the world, Gus wanted a dog. Six years ago, when they'd moved from Michigan to Tokyo for Dad's work, they'd had to leave their golden lab, Angel, with their cousins. Gus had really missed Angel, but he was so young then—just starting kindergarten— he survived. Jackie, however, who was in second grade at the time, had cried for Angel every night for months.

"Someone would have to take it out for walks two—three times a day. No matter what the weather, first thing in the morning, get dressed, wait for the elevator, go all the way down to ground level, *nineteen floors*, take the dog somewhere to poop, scoop it up, put it in a bag, find a trashcan . . ." his father made the sound of an exaggerated shudder before going on with the sequence " . . . wait for the elevator while all the school kids in the whole building are coming down, miss the bus, have to take the train . . ."

"Oh, come on, Charlie," interrupted Mom. "Don't be so negative. Just think of all the love a dog gives. Don't try to kid me; I know how much you miss Angel. I'm sure we can manage, between the four of us."

Slipping off his shoes, Gus agreed. At eleven and thirteen, he and Jackie would certainly be able to take care of a dog, even on the nineteenth floor of a high-rise in the center of Tokyo. They just had to convince Dad, he thought, as he set his sneakers side-by-side in the genkan shoe closet.

"Between the three of you, you mean. I won't be picking up dog poop. And just think of the expense," continued Dad. "The initial price tag is nothing compared to what it would really cost, with vet bills, food, grooming, and boarding every time we travel. One summer alone would be thousands of dollars."

"Oh, that's ridiculous. I'll get us some real numbers," said Mom, and Gus felt his heart give a little leap of hope.

The next day, Gus had aikido class in the middle school gym after school, so he rode the late bus, which was not unusual. The late bus route was different from the regular school bus route; it went all over the Tokyo metropolis and had fewer stops than the regular morning and afternoon bus that picked them up and dropped them off right at their apartment building. Most students then had to walk or take the subway to get home from the late bus stop, but it was totally worth it since it made after-school activities possible.

Gus had a good life, he would freely admit. Being an expat kid meant he got to do things other kids didn't get to do, like learn a language firsthand, vacation in Saipan, and tons of other stuff. But there were downsides, like not really feeling that you have a home, and always watching friends move away—and not having a dog.

The walk home took him right past *Zoo*, spelled in English on the sign. The tiny store sold a wide variety of animals, rotating them around their other locations. There was always something new. Or *someone*, as Gus preferred to think of the guest animals.

Mom had introduced him and his sister to the little pet store during those first lonely weeks when they were missing Angel so much. Ever since, he'd stopped in at least once a week. His parents were worried the staff would be annoyed—little foreigner kid coming in all the time and never buying anything. He wasn't the only expat kid to frequent the neighborhood pet store, but he was one of the few to stay in Japan long enough to learn enough Japanese to begin speaking with the staff, mostly pretty young women who were all really nice—and loved animals. As no one in the store knew more than a few words of English, Gus was taking the chance more and more to practice his budding Japanese when he'd stop by on the way home to check on the dogs.

Sometimes there were farm animals, like lambs, rabbits, a rooster, or even a piglet, which always seemed oddly exotic to Gus here, where pavement and skyscrapers defined the landscape. He liked the turtles, would always glance at the fish, and generally avoided the various tropical birds that rotated through, with their vicious looking beaks and tiny anklet chains to prevent escape. The kittens were cute enough, but Gus gravitated to the puppies, with their soft rounded bellies, sharp little teeth, and pleasant puppy breath.

The best thing about *Zoo* these days was Justice, the white bulldog who apparently lived in the shop. Justice stood at the doorway and greeted him when he arrived. Gus thought of Justice as *his* dog, in a way. After a few minutes of petting the big white dog, (he loved to be scratched behind the ears), Gus would make his way over to the cages where the puppies stayed, and Justice would follow him. If the object of his curiosity was on the lowest rack, and Gus would kneel down in order to visit with the puppy, Justice would push up next to him with his massive bulk and practically sit on him. This just made Gus want a dog of his own all the more.

After the conversation he'd overheard yesterday, Gus thought there might actually be a chance he could be getting a dog soon. He felt a serious sense of purpose, looking around the store. It was an important decision, and not necessarily an easy one. Dogs were different from each other; you had to choose the *right* dog. With about a dozen different breeds of puppies in the various cages, Gus was drawn to a large open-topped pen near the front of the cramped store. As he and Justice approached, the five large pups went crazy with tail wagging, jumping around and rough-housing each other. He tried to read the sign written in katakana, the Japanese alphabet for borrowed words: *raburado-ru retoriba-*. *Huh? Two were black and three were blonde and all had big feet. Wow, they're so playful, what great dogs!* He looked at the sign again and the language light went on in his head. *Labrador Retriever*. They were all so cute; it would be hard to choose.

Justice got up and walked over to the smaller cages and Gus followed. A fluffy ball of grey fur was curled up next to a water dish in the first cage while right next door was a barking yipping flurry of movement. The white and brown puppy with the thumping tail was probably a couple months old and licked Gus's hand through the bars. When Gus turned away to look at the other dogs, the little guy called him back with incessant little barks. It took him a minute to figure out the name of the breed, written in katakana. *Jyakku rasseru teria*, he read. *Ah, Jack Russell Terrier*. Then, staring at the sign, he realized the price. *230,000 yen. What? No way, he thought in disbelief, calculating in his head—over two thousand dollars! Maybe Dad was right.* Gus knew Tokyo was supposed to be one of the most expensive international cities, but this was outrageous.

He looked over at the sign for the Labs and saw their price was 180,000 yen. Less than the Jack Russell but still crazy expensive. *Maybe Mom would know how to find a shelter. Maybe that was the plan,* he told himself, as he walked to the back of the store to visit the turtles.

When he stood back up, made difficult by the weight of his backpack, he could see through the rows of cages, a man was bent over in the doorway scratching Justice behind the ears. *It looks like Dad. It is Dad! What was he doing here?* Gus turned around and stared into the iguana tank, tuning his ears for Dad's voice.

Right away, Dad called one of the staff over and started asking questions in Japanese. How old? Where born? Shots? (at least that's what Gus thought he was saying). He couldn't make out the clerk's answers, could only hear her soft voice, and he couldn't tell which cage they were standing next to without turning around and giving himself away, but what did it matter? They hadn't discussed price. *Nedan*: the showstopper.

The iguanas darted about as if startled. Gus realized someone was standing next to him. He didn't dare move. "So you don't want a dog after all," said Dad, setting a hand on his shoulder. "You want a lizard? I'm surprised, but it might be easier than a dog."

Gus laughed. "Of course I want a dog, Dad, I just didn't want to distract you while you were trying to speak Japanese," he said in a kidding voice. Dad knew many more words than Gus, but his pronunciation was terrible. It was a running joke between them.

"Just so you know, this is going to be a birthday present for your mom. It's kind of a sensitive birthday year for her. Otherwise, we would wait till we moved back to Michigan." Gus recalled something he'd overheard. Dad had been teasing her about it, calling it "The Big Five-Oh" and "over the hill" until Mom, who was a couple years older than Dad, had snapped at him to "Shut up!" and had left the apartment with her skates and hadn't come back for hours.

"Let's take a look," said Dad, signaling the manager and walked toward the Jack Russell, who was yipping and circling his cage. Gus's joy matched the dog's. The manager stopped in front of the cage next to it, opened the door and pulled out the grey ball of fur and tried to hand it to Dad, who pulled his hands away and pushed Gus forward.

There was hardly any weight, only the softness of the curly grey fur; floppy ears, poofy tail. "What is he?" asked Gus.

"He's a toy poodle. They don't shed. And he's almost six months old, so he's discounted, and partly housetrained. What do you think?" asked Dad.

Gus glanced over at the Jack Russell, who stood there wagging his tail, quiet for once, waiting. He looked again at the little grey dog in his hands and watched him open his mouth wide in an adorable yawn while reaching out and stretching each of his long coltish legs. Gus couldn't help but smile back when the yawn was complete and he found himself looking into the bright-eyed, smiling puppy face of the cutest dog in the world.

"He's the one, Dad," was all he needed to say.

****

Thus began Cooper's life with the Williams family, though he came to them as a present for Mom, Gus thought of Cooper as his dog. Jackie, who was obsessed with fashion, laid her claim as well, sewing outfits for the cute little poodle to wear on his walks though some of them made him look like a girl. Gus thought Cooper handled the indignity well. The weird thing was Dad, who would come home from work and call out *"Tadaima,"* *I'm home*, the typical Japanese greeting when returning home, and Cooper would race to the genkan to welcome him, jumping around with joy, as if he'd been gone for weeks. "It's because I'm the *Big Dog*, the leader of the pack," explained Dad, and Gus wondered what that made him, *the little mutt brother?* But it didn't really bother him—sharing Cooper with the rest of his family—plenty of puppy love to go around.

"Cooper, roll over. Roll over, Cooper," said Gus, making a circle in the air, but the little gray toy poodle just sat looking up at him with his bright eyes, and his head cocked to the side. "Come on buddy, roll over... please?"

Cooper stretched out his front legs in front of him, first one and then the other, and then crossed them and lay his head down on his paws. It was incredibly cute, but it wasn't roll over.

"You're doing it wrong. All wrong. Jeez kid," said Jackie, breezing through in a sundress, her hair in a ponytail.

"Be my guest," he told her.

"Well, I'm not an expert, but wouldn't you start with something more basic, like sit or stay?" Cooper sat at Jackie's feet and looked up at her with an expectant expression on his cute little teddy bear face. Jackie shrieked and applauded. "Where are the treats? He's sitting. Gus, give him a treat."

Gus knew he looked like a dork, standing there empty-handed.

"I guess I need to do some research," he said.

"Wise boy," said his mom, on her way to a skating event. "May I suggest you inquire the Internet, and then see if *Zoo* has anything you need, and get to work with your trick training. Good luck. Cooper and I, we get along just fine without tricks. He walks nicely on the leash for me, I don't really have to give him any orders, it's like he just knows," she said, zipping shut her bag and throwing it over her shoulder. "Have fun, kids."

Dad said Cooper's only trick was pooping, and called him "Cooper, the Pooper" to aggravate Mom, but it really seemed to be true. *Sit, stay, come*—none of these; nor *beg, fetch,* or *roll over*. Gus kept trying though, stuffing his pockets with dog treats, he'd take Cooper on walks to nearby places where they could practice the training. Cooper always attracted attention, often from girls, but all sorts, really. Taking Cooper out usually meant Gus would be practicing his Japanese.

Being a non-shedding dog meant Cooper needed regular haircuts. A no-brainer, since *Zoo* provided grooming services. Gus regularly picked up or dropped off Cooper for his grooming and occasional boarding, buying dog food and whatever Cooper needed, so he was visiting *Zoo* as often as before. Cooper loved going to *Zoo*, and tolerated Justice pretty well. Gus watched Justice sniff Cooper and realized their size ratio was probably a factor of ten. He thought, *isn't it weird about dogs, how different they can be and yet they're all still dogs?*

He wasn't quite sure where he wanted to go with this profound thought, but he knew it had something to do with the many different types of people he saw every day who seemed to get along just fine on the micro-level, person-to-person, but whose countries did not.

Mom bought a sturdy carrier bag for Cooper so they could take him on the train. Cooper would get all excited when the bag would come out, and would get in it all by himself. They would take him on the train, exploring far-flung suburbs with Cooper on a leash. When he got tired, or in places where walking him wasn't practical, like in crowds, Mom would tuck him into this little cloth carrier she had that attached to her front like a little baby. After attaining his full adult growth, Cooper was only four and a half kilograms, about ten pounds, but strangers often mistook him for a puppy he was so cute. Young Japanese women would always say "*kawaii,*" *cute*, when they saw him, drawing it out with a little squeak at the end, and try to take his picture. Gus noticed his dad especially enjoyed the chance to practice his Japanese when walking Cooper. Even though Gus and Jackie had vowed to help, it turned out that it was mostly Mom who took care of him, feeding him, making sure he got his walks, taking him to the vet, and to *Zoo* for grooming. Summer vacations were always a concern, but Mom worked it out, one or the other of her Japanese skater friends being willing to take care of Cooper for the few weeks they went back to the states every summer.

****

Four years passed, and by some corporate miracle, ten years after moving there, the Williams family was still living in Tokyo. It was the fall of Jackie's senior year of high school, and Gus's sophomore year, when tragedy struck.

Gus wasn't there when it happened, he was hanging out with his buds in Harajuku. Mom always invited him to go with her on these all-day group skates out of town, and sometimes he'd join, so he knew the scene. It meant getting up early, taking a long train ride to get to the start point of the skate, then several hours and kilometers of in-line skating with the group, and finally returning on a long train ride back. The Bunka-No-Hi skate took advantage of a national holiday in the middle of the week when many of Mom's skater friends were off school and work. Gus knew he should take the opportunity to practice his Japanese, but at fifteen, he would much rather sleep in and then hang out with his friends. Mom was really into it, though, these were her friends, and she was passionate about trying to improve her Japanese. She always said the exercise was just frosting on the top. That Wednesday morning she left before anyone else was awake.

Hours later, the way Dad tells it, he was walking with Cooper in a park some distance from home, when he got the call.

"Charlie, I broke my leg."

Of course, Dad thought she was kidding, or something. Nobody fractures their leg skating. Shoulders and wrists, sure— each of which Mom had already broken, but a leg—no.

"Would I kid about this?" she had shouted back and handed the phone away as the ambulance arrived there on the trail. Dad got the directions from the skaters, went home, got the car, and drove several hours to the small rural hospital in the next prefecture, taking Cooper along for company.

They didn't get back into Tokyo until after dark, and rather than take her straight to the hospital that night, Dad gave in to Mom's pleas and brought her home. Dad called when he was close to the apartment building and Jackie and Gus went down to the garage to help him get her up to the apartment.

Whenever Gus thinks about it now, he gets sick to his stomach. Mom was lying across the back seat of the car, her right leg encased in a primitive splint, her face pale and contorted with pain. Cooper was right there, nestled between Mom and the seat back. Mom managed a weak smile when Gus scooped the little gray poodle up and out.

"Good boy," she mumbled.

They had a heck of a time getting her out of the car—they kept hurting her. The broken leg wasn't very well immobilized, and every little movement caused her to cry out or catch her breath. *How would they ever get her into the elevator?* Jackie had the brilliant idea to go back up to the apartment and bring down the stool on rollers, so they waited while she did that, Mom gritting her teeth with tears on her face, hanging half in the car and half out, Cooper sticking to her like glue.

Mom balanced on the edge of the rolling stool while Gus tried his best to hold the busted leg steady, Dad pushed and Jackie dealt with doors and obstacles. That night, Cooper slept on Mom's bed, curled up next to a contraption of boxes and pillows Dad put there to try to keep her leg from moving. Cooper may have been the only one who slept that night.

In the morning, Gus got himself up as usual, while Dad tried to fill Mom's role of prying Jackie out of bed. His sister was still in the shower when he had already dressed, eaten a bowl of cereal, refilled his water bottle and put his backpack in the genkan. He stood in his parents' bedroom doorway and saw that Mom's eyes were closed. Cooper raised his head and looked at him with sleepy eyes, yawned, stretching out his longish legs, and proceeded to stretch out his entire body, making himself a "long dog" as Dad always said. Gus tiptoed around the bed and gingerly lifted Cooper off the covers, giving him a hug in the process. He noticed Dad must have slept on the sofa last night, and now he saw why. Even the slight change in the bed from him lifting off Cooper's tiny body had made Mom wince.

"Thanks, honey," she mumbled, her eyes closed. Thus began his practice of taking Cooper down for a walk before going to school each morning. A practice that would continue until Mom could take over again. Which would be longer than any of them ever expected.

Dad kept them updated that day via text, and was still at the hospital with Mom when Gus was on his way home on the late bus. He hoped the doctors and nurses spoke English and they knew their stuff. *Surely she would need surgery.* He hurried past *Zoo* with just a wave to Justice, who stood, tail wagging, guarding the doorway with his solid white bulk. Without Mom there, Cooper would be waiting to go out.

Hours later, after they'd gotten their own dinner, they heard Dad come in. "*Tadaima*" he called out as usual, *I'm home.*"

The report was perplexing. They didn't do surgery yet. They put her in traction. And no, it wasn't an English speaking hospital. Dad drove her to the institution recommended by the doctor from the emergency room up north, and it wasn't till they'd spent some time there that they realized it was a mistake. But she refused to be moved, wanting to avoid more pain and trouble.

Gus looked up "skeletal traction" on the Internet and the pictures made him feel woozy. He turned off the computer and plugged his phone into the charger and saw he had a text from Mom.

I'm ok. Thanks for taking care of Cooper

No problem. I'll come see you tomorrow.

Night.

Night.

The traction apparatus was as bad as Gus feared; they'd rammed a metal spike through her heel bone and attached it to a stirrup and ropes that ran up and down through pulleys, eventually to iron weights hanging free of the bed. Altogether, it stuck out past the normal length of the bed by half a meter, about eighteen inches. They had her in a crowded six-bed ward with five older Japanese ladies. The curtain was drawn around her bed. She looked so small and helpless, but her face lit up when she opened her eyes and saw him.

During that first visit, something happened that Gus would never be able to forget. He was sitting at the bedside chatting with his mom when there was a noise, the bed shuddered and his mom's face contorted all out of whack and she groaned really loud. Somebody, it turned out it was a medical student, had banged into the unseen dangling weights through the curtain, sending a horrible spasm of pain through Mom's shattered bones as the traction abruptly lost tension. Gus could see the broken bone moving around under her skin. It was horrible. The obvious solution was to keep the curtains open. But every time he came, it was always closed.

"Mom, why is this curtain always pulled? Do you want it this way?"

"No, I don't especially, but it's okay since I can see out the window."

"Well, I'll open it then."

"They'll just close it again."

"Who? The nurses? Why?"

"I don't know honey. I suppose it upsets the other patients to see me like this," she said, making Gus feel bad for her all over again. And then she laughed. "Six years in Japan, and you are still asking "Why," she said, smiling.

He leaned against the windowsill and thought of another solution: *angle the bed.*

He should be able to do it himself. On closer inspection, he saw that the bottom end of the heavy hospital bed rested on specially made blocks, to keep Mom from sliding down with the constant pull from the traction.

"I'm going to need some help, I can't move it by myself," he told Mom, appraising the sturdy bed with its mantle of heavy orthopedic framing. It would take at least three people, he guessed.

"Move what? The bed? Oh, don't move the bed, Gus, honey. Everything hurts. They've bumped into me four times already today. I just…" she trailed off.

****

Gus wasn't satisfied Mom was getting good care. He visited often, but not every day. It was hard to see her in pain. She said the nurses were stingy with the pain medicine. The doctor had ordered it for her, but she had to ask and ask to get it. The nurses made her feel like an addict whenever she put her call light on and acted like it was their job to make her wait longer. Due to being in pain all the time, she couldn't get any sleep. He had heard her telling Dad about the "culture" of the Japanese hospital and compared it to the hospital she used to work at in Michigan.

"The doctors are fine, but the nurses are only here to wait on the doctors and keep order. They don't have any autonomy.

They do nothing to prevent complications or promote comfort. No skin care, no range of motion, and they certainly don't care about pain control," she had complained to Dad. "They're all over me if they hear me talking on my cell phone, but they're fine to let me lie moaning in pain. It's like where nursing was in the '60s and '70s in the U.S. I guess I shouldn't be surprised; it goes along with their patriarchal system. But Japan is so advanced in so many ways—just my luck, always on the wrong side of the bed," she said and gave a weak laugh. Gus sat at her bedside, thinking about the problem of people banging into the weights.

"*Konbanwa*," came a deep voice, "Good Evening", and Shige-san's bright face popped around the edge of the curtain along with his girlfriend, Tomi-chan.

"*Ikaga desuka*?" *How are you*, they asked Mom, concern written all over the faces. Mom smiled big. "I'm fine... I mean, *dai jyo bu*," she answered.

Perfect. Shige-san was a big guy—strong. Gus explained about moving the bed, to avoid the clumsy staff. Shige bent down and assessed the bed frame and the blocks. They talked about how the bed would end up angled toward the middle of the window. Before they could make a move, a nurse came in. It was the one Mom called *Nurse Ratchet*, though Gus was pretty sure that wasn't her name.

She was a pretty Japanese woman wearing a white dress uniform complete with white hose, shoes, and a nursing cap. Tomi asked her a question; Gus could tell it was about moving the bed. The nurse glared at Mom for a moment and responded to Shige and Tomi in rapid formal Japanese of which Gus could catch very little. She went on and on, rarely looking at Mom and never at Gus, and when she was done, she bowed quickly and backed out.

Everyone was silent. They looked from one to another. Shige put a finger to his lips and motioned Gus over to the right foot of the bed. Tomi took hold of the hanging weights; with such a light touch Mom never flinched.

"*Ki wo tsukete*," she said, *Be careful*, and Shige and Gus moved the bed ever so gently until it stood at a respectable angle from the wall, the weights clearing the curtain.

"*Arigato*," Mom said, again and again, *Thank you*.

It stayed that way for three days, until the next time Nurse Ratchet worked. Gus couldn't keep that problem solved, but he did pin a sign to the other side of the curtain, which was better than nothing. He also helped Dad rig up a way for Mom to get the Internet on her computer, unbeknownst to the staff. Certainly, Nurse Ratchet wouldn't approve of that either.

Gus and Jackie took turns visiting every other day after school, bringing Mom treats like little cups of ice cream from the 7-11. Usually, they would play cards, or she would help him study for a test. The hospital wasn't all that far from one of the late bus stops, so Gus worked it out with Jackie for him to visit on the days he had aikido after school. Then home was less than two kilometers, about a mile, which Gus could walk in twenty minutes, even though it was uphill. It was fine fall weather and good exercise. The only trouble was poor little Cooper, who would sniff the air and look around for Mom when he'd finally get home.

On the twelfth day after the accident, the doctors finally did surgery on Mom's leg. They put a titanium rod inside the tibia bone and secured it with screws. Gus was just glad that wretched traction was finally out of the room and hoped this would help the pain a lot. Instead of putting on a cast, the plan was to use a special non-weight-bearing brace, but it would take a few days to get that custom made.

On the Sunday before Thanksgiving, Dad asked Gus to help him with a little project. Gus had wanted to sleep in, but figured things were hard enough for Dad with Mom in the hospital, it wouldn't hurt him to help with whatever it was. But as he brushed his teeth, he couldn't help but notice Jackie's closed bedroom door. Fall of senior year was notoriously tough with all the college applications and everything, but Gus was still annoyed that Jackie got to sleep. Dad was waiting in the genkan. "Come on Pooper!" he called. The little gray toy poodle came running, his teddy bear face hopeful, his ears perked up and tail held high. Yesterday, Gus had taken him to *Zoo* for grooming and they had sure done him up cute. Dad handed Gus the leash. *Yay, Cooper was going!*

"Hold still, buddy," he said to the fluffy gray moving target. Cooper stood still and let Gus snap the harness on his little body. On the walk to the hospital, Gus filled Dad in on school and life. They had to stop a couple of times for people to meet Cooper—a young mother pushing a toddler in a stroller kept telling the kid to look, *"Wan-chan"* she said, which means puppy, and a little further on, an elderly couple. *"Kawaii,"* cute, they both said, and Gus picked Cooper up so the lady could pet him. Her smile grew, *"Kawaii,"* she said again.

"Cooper brings joy to everyone he meets," he observed to Dad, who rolled his eyes.

Dad told Gus about his work, and how his boss was pressuring him to take a business trip to India but he was trying to put it off.

"You can go, don't worry. I'll take care of things here," Gus told Dad, who smiled and patted his back. "Thanks, son. I'll keep that in mind."

Gus and Cooper waited outside on a little patio while Dad went up to Mom's room. Gus occupied the time trying to get Cooper to learn a trick, but he was too excited—kept running around and glancing toward the door Dad went into. Eventually, the door opened, and Dad brought Mom out in a wheelchair, her leg propped up and sticking out. Cooper whimpered and strained at the leash as she came down the ramp. For such a little guy, he sure was strong.

"Cooper, oh Cooper," exclaimed Mom, her arms outstretched, her cheeks wet, and soon the wiggly dog was on her lap and licking her face.

There was a shout from far away, then more voices closer, and a low rolling sound. Gus knew that sound, and so did Mom. Her eyes opened wide as she looked out at the street. Around the corner came the skaters led by Shige and Tomi. It was Sunday after all; the day Mom usually joined her group for the cross-town skate. With her friends gathered around her, everybody speaking Japanese, Mom smiled laughed. He guessed there were at least a couple dozen skaters. Since he sometimes went skating with Mom, Gus knew almost everyone; Toichi, Yuya, Machi, pretty Keiko... huh? Jackie? His sister skated up and T-stopped right in front of Gus. She was wearing a hoody over shorts with tights—no knee pads.

"I thought you were sleeping," he said.

"Fooled you," she said with an evil smile and turned to Mom, giving Dad a high five in passing. After leaning over the wheelchair for a quick hug, his sister skated over to a bench, followed by an entourage of three of the slalom guys. Gus watched, shaking his head.

Cooper yipped and wagged his tail from the center of it all on Mom's lap, cutest dog in the world.

****

Gus woke to a rainstorm the first Friday in December, the day Mom was scheduled to come home from the hospital. During second period, physics, Gus noticed the rain had stopped and the sun was out. He was on his way home on the bus when he got the text from Dad that Mom was home and all was well. He was kind of surprised to notice he had actually been worried. *What could happen? It was just a matter of getting back to normal now.* Soon, he got a text from Mom.

Cooper was so glad to see me.

I bet.

He piddled.

TMI, mom

He settled back in the bus seat to watch the familiar scenery go by from the elevated freeway—tops and balconies of mid-rise residential buildings. As he watched for the usual oddities, the roof with all the pink plastic flamingos, the building painted to look like King Kong was climbing up the side, he wondered when Mom would start cooking again.

****

Later that weekend…"Yes, Dad. Yes, Dad. I know, Dad," said Jackie, "Hey, let me put you on speaker-phone so you can remind us all for the hundredth time… oh, okay. Well, have a good flight. Let us know when you make it to Bangalore. Everything is fine," she clicked off and looked around at Mom who leaned on the wall resting on her crutches, and Gus, holding Cooper on the leash. They had all just come out of the elevator on their floor and were standing outside the door of their apartment when Dad called. They'd taken a short walk in the neighborhood, but it had turned into quite a task, what with Mom not being very skilled with her crutches yet, especially on stairs, and Cooper and his leash getting in the way. No wonder Mom was tired. They got the door open and she crutched it straight to the living room. Cooper jumped up on the sofa with her and no one shooed him off.

"At least you're moving around, that's what you're supposed to do, right?" Gus asked her, watching Jackie undo the Velcro straps and help her off with the long-leg brace. He was glad she had leggings on under the brace; he didn't want to see the scars. But the brace was interesting. "Did you have a choice of color, Mom? I like the blue."

"Yes, I like the blue too, or I did. Now I associate it with the brace and pain. I think it might be fitting too tight. It even hurts when it's off now. Anyway, I need a break from it. Jackie, can you bring me my pain pills?"

Gus picked up the two parts of the brace, which basically served as an exoskeleton; a metal piece protruded under the molded foot.

He fit the custom brace to the front and back of his own leg and threaded the wraps. He grabbed Mom's crutches, tried to walk and almost toppled. "What the... how do you do this?"

"My other shoe is built up, to make up for the non-weight bearing bar at the bottom," she said, and he saw what she meant. The extension was a shock absorber for the leg.

"I'm going to rest a bit," she said, her voice small, her eyes closed. Gus felt a pang of worry for his mom. "I hope you have your homework done. Tomorrow's Monday," she added, sounding more like herself.

****

Gus dreamed he was on the school bus watching the apartment balconies and rooftops go by. On one of the rooftops was a curly gray toy poodle that looked like Cooper running around barking. As the bus got closer and closer, he saw it was definitely Cooper, he could even see the purple collar and bone-shaped metal nametag. He was barking and barking, incessantly. Running around and around on the roof.

"Cooper, stop it," said Gus, but he kept on barking.

"Cooper, what's wrong with you?" it was his sister's voice.

Gus's eyes snapped open and the barking continued. He got out of bed and stumbled into the hall. Jackie stood outside her door wearing a T-shirt and boxers, her long hair wild. Cooper, his little body at high alert, stood in the open doorway of the master bedroom barking up at her. Jackie took a swipe at him and he ran into Mom's room. She disappeared behind him and Gus followed her into the bedroom. The bed was a pile of pillows and blankets, otherwise empty. The big picture window showed the Tokyo Tower in all its brilliant orange glory. *2 a.m. and all is not well,* he thought.

"She's in here," Jackie called to him. "Come help me."

Mom sat on the side of the bathtub, slumped and gasping. Gus was terrified for her but glad to see she was dressed. He ducked out and came back with the rolling stool. They used it to get Mom out of the bathroom and to the bed. She was like a rag doll, super weak, couldn't catch her breath. Gus put her legs up on the bed and she leaned back against a pile of pillows. Jackie set to fastening the blue brace, securing each Velcro strap. What was happening? Mom looked at Gus and said something to him but she only moved her lips, no sound came out.

"Get her things. Cell phone, charger. Purse. She's going back," ordered Jackie. "Now." Gus ran around getting stuff while Jackie got her clothes sorted out. Mom was insistent, "use the plastic bag from the hospital." It had the name and address of the hospital printed on it along with a big green cross.

"I don't want to go back there," she rasped, "but they know me."

He wondered if he should try to call Dad or wait. Minutes later, they were all standing outside next to the street. Cooper was taking a poop when the taxi stopped and Jackie got Mom and her stuff into the back and talked to the driver. When the taxi drove away with just Mom in it, Gus didn't know what to say.

"How's she going to do this?" he stammered.

"She knows what she's doing. If you call an ambulance, it causes all kinds of trouble; they have to get permission from the hospital to go there. But if you just show up in a taxi…"

"Okay, I get it. But she's all alone," said Gus.

"Mom said we can go to school tomorrow. Or not. I guess she left it up to us. Come on, let's go in and see if we can get a hold of Dad.

This time was different. They put her in the ICU. She had oxygen and was surrounded by lots of IV's and machines; blood thinners and clot busters, medicine for breathing, shots for pain. The heart doctor stopped by often and Gus was happy to hear him speak English. "Dr. Fujii went to school in Boston," said Mom, through her oxygen mask. "He's up on all the latest stuff. He's taking good care of me," she reported.

Dad barely made it to India before turning around and flying back to Tokyo. It was a full week before they moved Mom out to the regular floor, and this time put her in a room of her own.

Gus was there that day and helped push the bed. All the nurses from the ICU bowed and waved goodbye. Everything was fine till they got to the regular floor and saw Nurse Ratchet standing at the desk.

"Not her again," he mumbled. But it was a nice room, just big enough for one bed and a small refrigerator. It had a different view of the same construction site. *Hopefully, Mom won't have to stay so long this time;* Gus thought and vowed to visit her every day.

****

One day, popping into his mom's room after school, Gus came upon a strange scene. A doctor was sitting on her bed and seemed to be rubbing something on Mom's chest under the covers. Gus tried to duck out before anyone saw him, but he stumbled over the trashcan, making a clatter.

"Gus, come over here, look at this," said Mom, and asked the doctor to show him the screen. Mom never missed a chance for learning, and he did find the images fascinating, if he could forget for a moment it was his mom's heart. As the doctor moved the little probe around, the various chambers of the heart burst into view, always in motion.

"So, do you think you'd like to work in healthcare, Gus?" asked Mom.

"Not on your life," he said, and then frowned at his choice of words. He caught her eye.

"Sorry, Mom, I gotta go... homework," and he practically ran out of the room. He skipped going to the hospital the next couple of days and texted Mom that he was busy with homework. Dad went every day and said she was doing fine medically, but seemed to be getting more and more down in the dumps.

Gus couldn't really explain why he was staying away, but he figured it had something to do with being fifteen and having his mom in the hospital so much. She'd always been the one to take care of everything. Even after she broke her leg and through all those days of traction, and then the surgery, and then the rehab, Mom had mostly stayed positive. But this hospitalization, with the blood clot and the lung problem and now the heart complications—all on top of the still broken leg—it was just too much.

Gus decided to take matters into his own hands, literally. The next day, as soon as he got home from school, he took Cooper out as usual, but this time, they kept walking. Before they got to the hospital, Cooper stopped and looked up at Gus, the sign his little legs were tired. Gus was prepared. He removed the little dog's harness and leash, put them in his pocket and tucked Cooper into the front carrier pouch he was wearing under his jacket. When he got to the hospital grounds, he carefully zipped the jacket up to his neck. "Now you be quiet, Cooper. Don't give me away," he said into his jacket and strode into the lobby.

He moved to the back of the elevator as more and more people packed in. The doors closed, and he noticed a tall white coated man standing next to him, looking down into his coat front at Cooper. Gus stiffened, waiting. The doors opened and closed on each floor and the man stood right next to him. Finally, it was just the two of them, Gus moved a little away from the man in the white coat and wondered what would happen next.

"*Kawaii*," said the man, and got off at the next stop. It was Mom's floor, so Gus had to get off too, but he hung back as the doctor walked down the hall and turned a corner. Gus began to release the breath he was holding.

Standing at the nurses' station, was Nurse Ratchet, watching him.

"*Konichiwa*," they both said at once. He was relieved when she turned away.

Mom was lying in the bed, staring off into space. She looked up and smiled when he came in. He made sure she was alone and then went back and shut the door to the hall. He turned around and unzipped his jacket. Mom saw Cooper and gave a little shriek. Cooper saw Mom and gave a little woof.

"Sh, sh, sh," they both shushed him, laughing. Gus put the excited gray toy poodle on the bed, who went straight to Mom and covered her face with puppy kisses.

"Oh, Gus, you shouldn't have," she said, happy tears on her cheeks.

After a while, he tucked Cooper back in the pouch, zipped up his jacket and kissed his mom on the top of her head.

He made it safely outside and walked down the street to a bench next to a bus stop where he sat down and took Cooper out of the pouch and secured his harness and leash for the walk home.

Cooper was wagging his tail. Someone was walking towards them. It was Nurse Ratchet. Gus shirked into his coat, hoping she would just keep walking.

She stopped. Cooper sat, looking up at her, his head cocked to one side, his little pink tongue poking out like a goofy smile.

"*Kawaii,*" she said, in a high voice, drawing out the last syllable like a teenage girl.

A second later she saw it was Gus and an odd expression washed over her face, as full awareness dawned—and then—a tiny little smile.

"*Arigatou,*" said Gus, and he turned and walked towards home as fast as he could, following Cooper, who pranced along on his leash, tail wagging, bringing cuteness and joy.

10.
Damn Dog Died
Edward Ahern

Damn Dog Died.
Twelve years feeding and walking together.
Seeking touches from each other.
Well-spoken, wordless glances.
Graceful dance partners slowing in rhythm.
Damn Dog Died

11.

Dog Days of Autumn
Sharon Frame Gay

This is the time of year when all things seem possible. Mornings are misty, filled with promise, brimming with delightful scents on the breeze. I catch the trace of a female fox; cutting across our creek on the way to her den, a musty smell mixed with mother's milk, quick little prints across the muddy bank, then up into the woods, disappearing like a ghost trail. Scents stay longer on the lower notes near the ground, held in place by dew. I feel frisky, almost like a puppy again. Almost, except that there is something missing. There are times when I still gaze down the road, looking for him.

My name is Razz. Short for Razzmatazz, a name my people gave me, when I still had my milk teeth, torn from my mother's teat, carried home in a cardboard box. Those early days with my litter are cloudy in my mind. I belong here, now, to these people, the boy and girl, the woman. My family. And I belong to him, strong and kind, smelling of male sweat, pressed shirts, mints and a bit of tobacco. I am a Golden Retriever. Proud to wave my tail like a flag, proud to serve, to protect. I remember him saying something just like that, when he left that day, duffle flung over his shoulder, tears in his eyes, the long blast from the waiting train down by the station, mournful, foreboding. The woman cried hard and held him for the longest time on our front porch. Then, when he stepped off on to the sidewalk, she threw her arms around me, and cried some more. I was already an older dog, then, but I stood as tall as I could, supporting her weight, head up, stoic, standing for her as long as she needed me. I was there for the children, too. When he left he said, "watch over all of them, Razz", and I did.

I don't know where he went, but a lot of the men around here went with him. I kept hearing some words over and over again that sound like "Dubbya dubbya two" and strange names like Italy, Germany, France. Letters tumbled through the slot in our front door, smelling foreign, exotic, inviting. They crackled under my nose, and I was tempted to rip them up and eat them but I know the woman wanted them, waited for them, and somewhere, deep under the envelope, beneath the ink, I smelled him. I wagged my tail and looked out the window for him. I whined, scratched at the floor, until the children called me away. "Come Razz, come play fetch" and we raced out the door and into the alley, tearing down the pathways after an old tennis ball that had seen better days.

The seasons went by, but I never forgot him. I missed him, wanted to play with him, feel his strong arms around me, around the woman, the little boy and girl. I have now taken it upon myself to raise the children. Patient and kind, I sleep beside them on the bed, licking their faces and cuddling up so they stay warm during the cool nights. I growl at the post man, the delivery man, anybody who enters the yard and walks to our front door. It's my duty, and I take it seriously. I am the man of the house now, me, old Razz, and I am keeping it safe.

One day I growled at a young man on a bicycle as he pedaled up to our garden gate. He smelled of sadness and stress, office buildings and the oil of old typewriters. "Down boy", he said to me, reaching into his bag and pulling out a yellow piece of paper. "There's a good dog now" he murmured as he sidled past me. I sensed no danger on him, and allowed him to pass, walk up the stairs, knock on the door, and speak to the woman. "Telegram", he said gently, and the woman fell to her knees, keening, reaching for the door jamb. My hackles went up as I stalked up the steps, bristling. What was this person doing to her? She was crying, reaching for me. "Oh Razz, he's gone missing! Missing in action"! I don't know what that meant, but I know that her heart was beating hard as she wrapped her arms around my neck.   The young man backed down from the steps, away from us, and I set to barking ferociously at him - "get off my property", I howled in outrage. "Leave my people alone".   Then I turned back towards her, and the children, as the whole world seemed to grow dim. Something happened. I didn't understand. Where was he? I need him here to help. I need him to hold us all.   Then, I set my tail, held up my head, and got back to the business of raising this family. Just me. Just good old Razz.

Time went by, and with it the seasons. The children and I spent many lazy summer days in the creek out back, swimming and catching bullfrogs and crawdads. I sat on the bank in the sun to dry off, my fur smelling like wet wool, watching the kids as they ran back and forth along the rocks, buckets in hand, the woman not far away, sitting on a blanket, staring into the distance. Autumn came again, and I took the children to the school around the corner every day, my tail a plume as we stepped lively along the sidewalk, catching up with other children, all the little kids reaching down to grab my fur, patting me on the head.   I stood like a good dog.

Then came Christmas, my favorite time of the year.   There were dog treats, and a new bed, too, and cookies that somehow found their way off the plate in the kitchen. I was stealthy. Took just one or two. Oh, but they were like happiness in my mouth! The best! And the tree in the living room smelled like the outdoors - Frasier pine, sap, birds. When I was a young pup, I lifted my leg on it, spraying my scent, just like I do outside. I got into trouble. The man dragged me out of the room by my collar and pushed me out the door. I was mortified.   From then on, I treated that strange tree with respect.

Spring came, and with it baby bunnies for me to chase. I never tried to catch them. Just gave them a little thrill as I escorted them out of the yard. The earth smelled like birth, the sun on my coat felt like it had crept closer. But still, the woman sat, waiting, staring out the window, her hand on my head. "Good Razz," she would say "there's my old friend". I lay down on the floor beside her as she cried. My muzzle is turning white, my bones ache a bit, eyesight not as good as it once was, but one thing I can surely do is cry with her. I am getting old and starting to worry how long I will be able to be here, to take care of them. I whimper like a puppy.

And now it is autumn again. The air is sharper. Sounds travel farther through the leafless trees. Even the lonely sound of the train down at the station lingers on the air a bit longer, its whistle piercing the sky.

Something made me feel itchy deep in my soul when I heard that whistle. Not the kind of itch that a flea gives off, but the feeling of unrest when I catch something on the breeze. A scent. Like smoke and mints, only from far, far away, and something else, too. Something else that excited me, raised the hackles on my back. I barked to be let out. I raced across the porch and down the stairs, turned in circles, nose up, sniffing the air, growling. Whining. Ears cocked, eyes everywhere.

And then... I saw him, walking down the sidewalk. Slower, much slower than he used to walk, limping a bit. The duffle flung over his shoulder, each step bringing him closer to me, to us, to the rest of our lives. The screen door slammed and the woman walked out behind me, peered up the sidewalk, a quick intake of breath, a stifled sob.

"Razz!" he cried. I let out a bark that shook the last leaves off the trees and ran into his arms. It is autumn, and all things are possible.

12.
DoG: Man's Best Friend
Outstanding Dogs
Thomas Tabor

Over my life this far I've known some remarkable dogs. But why have I written dog with a capital 'G' at the end? Read on please.

The first dog I remember was old Baskom, a somewhat reddish brown one, who may have been part Irish setter. He was brownish red with medium long hair, round head, longish nose, and pleasant mouth with floppy ears. He was the pet of all the family in Oak Park, Illinois and belonged to my Aunt, Uncle, and both cousins, but after the death of Nanoo, Uncle Al's aunt, I think, our family moved to Nanoo's house.

Uncle Al went blind from T.B. of eye. A rare form spread only through careless use of face towels in men's collegiate dorm situation. His first seeing-eye-dog was a boxer named Chief, but when Uncle Al and Aunt Marion came to the family summer cottage on the Lake Michigan near Holland, Chief, having never seen sand, accidently ran my uncle into a tree he was so excited.

Our first dog Tzar is one we had in Detroit. Tzar was pure Boston terrier but a throwback to a brindle. He was with us till his death at age twenty.

Part Spitz, part Collie that was our last dog. Trixie had one bad habit she picked up from the Dutchess, a collie. After Dutchess died, Trixie became Queen of all Dogs on Devonshire Road, including Terry a big wire-haired terrier. When Trixie chased our cat back into our front yard, the cat jumped onto a low brick wall.

Trixie, who was a little bitch, interposed herself between our cat and the much larger dog Terry and showed an angry snarl of all her teeth while growling at Terry. Terry backed right on down, terrified of the much smaller female dog. Trixie was our last dog, and I found her dead out on the Southfield Road after she had been missing for two or three days.

We had no more dogs after Trixie's death, but we had at varying times a total of fifteen female cats.

There are numerous other dogs from Chihuahua, to Dobermans and Great Danes. But none can compare to the dogs I knew and grew up around.

Now d.o.G backwards spells God. Think about it, dog = God.

Yes, no, maybe, perhaps?

After thought, what if it man's best friend is his dog, why not man's best friend is his God!

13.
Dog
Renata Rzepecki-Dawidowicz

The dark deserted streets with abandoned homes falling down cascading to the overgrown weeds

Into this maze of forgotten homes appear our homeless dogs in packs for their very survival

They wander through this city living a meager existence in their short lives

Wanting to live they fight for life in these harsh circumstances

They have been let loose because their owners died or moved and the dogs are old now

Cars run them over as they search all over for food fighting with other dogs for left over crumbs

Catching viruses and disease if they are lucky enough not to eat rat poison that kills them

Into their world of despair come no kill animal rescue groups, a beacon of hope in their plight

If you want a dependable friend and can afford it these dogs will make loving companions

They understand what it is to be down and out and they will appreciate a good home

If you live alone and your partner has died they can guard you with their lives if intruders appear

This older woman was afraid to live alone when her husband died so she has this lovable big dog

She felt safe because this old dog with a limp paw would bark when someone was on her property

When the economy is bad there is strong competition between adopting a puppy or an old dog

Also these abandoned dogs have to be trained first and it does take time and money

There is a beginning and hopefully all shelters will be no kill so every animal has the same rights

We cannot pick and choose who should die: young, old sick, and a particular breed

Circumstances in their life gave them a hard road to travel in these forsaken streets

There are so many unfair circumstances for these homeless dogs but there is hope for them

Also the secret is out feral animals make very lovable pets because they never want to go back

No one does

14.
Doggedly Downtrodden
A.J. Huffman

The sound of dew, dripping from midnight's
trees echoed like a jackhammer, turned
my mind murky. I sacrificed comfort
for concealment, buried myself
in make-shift tunnel of blankets.
My Chihuahua thought I was playing, followed
me into downed blind. I laughed
as we began competing for prime folds
of stuffed satin. Somewhere in the distance,
a door slammed like a bible, a thud
that reverberated through our windless night.
My mood shifted, as if a branch
of something sinister grafted itself to my skin.
Before I could close my eyes to the idea,
a fresh set of shivers slivered down my spine.
I shut our fabric tunnel like a coffin, curled myself around
canine companion. Together we cowered
until dawn.

15.
For I Will Consider My Dog Chico
Betty Hartnett

Inspired by Christopher Smart's "For I Will Consider My Cat Jeffrey"
- Christopher Smart (1722-1771)

For I will consider my dog Chico

For he is brave in heart even when not in action

For he loves school children who love him in return

For he loves to lick their small warm hands as they giggle in response

For he loves to listen to them read and occasionally look at the pictures in their book

For he looks into the eyes of memory care residents as they pet him with unsteady hands

For he is eager for our daily treks with his nose to the ground and the new smells

For he prances as he walks in crisp and not so crisp morning air

For he glances back at me on our walks to check on what I'm not sure

For he sits at my side as I chat with neighbors on our walks

For he will run with me if I want to run

For he steps between the cats and young children who know not how to treat cats with respect

For he waits on the sofa if I am leaving and can't take him along

For he is always excited to go for a ride, though he knows not where we're going or for how long

For he sometimes sleeps in the car with his nose on the window glass

For he sometimes comes into the front seat of the car, especially after memory care visits

For he sometimes sits up straight as we drive looking from side to side at the scenery

For he sometimes sleeps soundly on the car seat trusting my driving to get us wherever safely

For he loves being scratched behind his ears and under his chin and on his belly

For he spends hours lying on the lawn near the flower garden as I weed and prune

For I will miss him when his dog days are done and I am still here

16.
Found In Translation
By Jon Moray

I came home early from work, opened up my front door, and found my loving beagle greeting me with a howling serenade and a whirlwind tail. As I ventured further in, I discovered my home fell victim to burglary. The house was pretty much in order except for my most valuable electronics, three flat screen TV's, two tablets and two laptops were gone. My wife's jewelry was also stolen.

I called 911 and dispatch sent an officer over within a half-hour. A slew of questions were asked, and I answered with stunned responses while my dog barked and howled unmercifully.

"There has been a rash of burglaries in this area the past few months," the officer announced, blandly. Two other investigators stopped by and dusted for fingerprints. The trio wrapped up their work, and the lead informed me there wouldn't be much luck in retrieving the stolen articles.

I called my wife at work and left a message on her extension and on her cell. She did say she was busy with meetings for most of the day when we ate breakfast that morning. I decided to leave her several text messages briefly explaining the terrible days' events.

I was lost in thought, and while writing my next text, my dog began to howl and bark at the front door. I quickly jumped to my feet, opened the door and saw my neighbor down the street, walking her dog past our house on the concrete walkway. I rendered a patronizing wave and went back into my house.

I rubbed my dog behind the ears and went back to my text draft. I sat down at the dining room table and noticed there was already text in the draft window.

"Get away from my yard, you mangy mutt," is what it read. I muttered the text repeatedly in wonder and at a major loss of understanding. *I didn't write that, why would I write anything like that*, I reasoned to myself. Suddenly, my beagle howled, and again directed at the front door. I went to investigate and found it was the mailman dropping off a package for me at the front door. I retrieved the package, acknowledged my dog by scrubbing his nape, and went back to my phone.

"Hurry up with your business and get out of here, Postman," is what it read this time. I looked at my phone and at my dog and volleyed my spies back and forth at them as I tried to piece together any sanity I had left in me. My wannabe detective fantasies were now becoming a reality and being put to the test. The dog barks and then I get words on my phone, and in English, no less. Somehow, someway, my audible text messaging application translates my dog's barks into real words. That's what I've come up with so far, but way too early to tell anyone for fear they would have me committed.

I paced the living room like I were part of some kind of unorganized line dance as my dog mimicked my steps, with his tongue wagging. I sat back down and peered at my phone and back at my tri-colored beagle.

"Gunner, do you know who robbed our home?" He barked once and tilted his head. I looked down at my phone, and it read, "yes." Just then the doorbell rang, and my dog barked, which was par for the course when the bell rings.

I ran over and opened the door. "Hi, I saw the police at your door, is everything alright?" asked Ms. Lacey, my neighbor next door that had just moved into the house beside me three weeks ago.

"My house got robbed," I said and invited her in. Gunner expressed his disapproval of her intrusion to no end while I tried to provide her with an explanation of what happened. I tried to silence my dog, but the more I tried, the more he fussed and I began to get an eerie feeling something wasn't right with his baying disapprovals.

I made my way over to my phone and saw a continuous string of words in the text draft window. "It's her. She's the one who robbed us. She fooled me with bacon treats to keep me occupied. She got in through the garage where she somehow knew the door code. She's the one." Just then, Gunner raced out the partially opened front door while I desperately followed in pursuit. Ms. Lacey trailed behind us.

Gunner bolted towards Ms. Lacey's front door, and his momentum sent him forcing the door open, over the threshold and into her home. I followed him in and to my surprise; all of my valuables were situated neatly on the floor in her living room. I called the police and learned Ms. Lacey was a career criminal that would bounce around from place to place, befriend neighbors and rob them blind. She knew my neighbors across the street worked during the day. After police got done with their work, my valuables were returned, and all was back to normal.

My wife got home from work and after filling her in on all the fantastic details of the day, I decided to feed dinner to my nose-to-the-ground, detective dog. I scooped up his portion of brown rice and chicken dog food and heard him bellow out a few barks. I looked at him and turned to my phone.

"C'mon, throw me a bone. I just solved a mystery. Give me the really good stuff you usually reserve for holidays and my birthday," read the text draft. I chuckled, showed the text contents to my wife, and did as my beagle requested.

17.
From Chico
Betty Hartnett

"I wished I was a horse, and I could lay my head over your neck."
~*Jean Valentine, The Older Man among Us*

I lie on a rug
While twenty-three first graders
Line up to pet me

Their hands are small
And soft, I lick them
They giggle

It's orientation to their
"reading to a dog" program
If I could sing, I would

18.
From Willow to Nome
John C. Mannone

The fourteen-dog Iditarod team of Kobuk and Husky dogs plowed through the tundra, and through the snows of the spruce forest, before reaching the whiteout-blizzard on Rainy Pass. They sledded down the mountain in a cold-blistered wind, not thinking about the race anymore, but hauling their fellow canine in the basket. Junior, exhausted and hypothermic from the storm, labored to breathe in the icy air. But soon, smoke chimney'd above the ridge and into the clouds—the team smelled hope among the soot and flurries. The wooden shelter loomed into view. When Junior was carried in to this "dog-drop," they whimpered—it sounded like prayers.

Grace, the alpha female, refused to eat. But when their musher had consoled her and then saw her brother stir under a heavy scotch plaid blanket, they ululated no elegy. Instead, they all celebrated with wild salmon lining their bowls; their icy tongues stabbing the fish, while their master washed down some caribou jerky with a bit of honey wine not yet turned to vinegar. The sour taste of defeat will not touch his lips, for Junior will live to run many more Alaskan trails... and win.

19.
Gunshot
Briana J. Weiss

The gophers this year were terrible. Tommy would take barely a step off the concrete patio before he found himself stumbling in a small hole created by one of the little rascals. Speaking of rascals, Tommy's huge lab Rascal was rarely seen without his snout shoved down one of those many tunnels. And when Tommy would gleefully run around the acreage and step in a hole or two, Rascal would be there to nudge him back up from the ground.

Every year it was a game for the two--Tommy would waddle along (walk, now; back then he waddled as any toddler would), after spying the little critters running around the yard, and Rascal would follow behind, as if cautious of the gophers. And at Tommy's cry of "There!" Rascal would pounce, even though both the large dog and the gopher knew the little boy's call was far too late. But the entertainment lasted for hours.

And as Tommy aged, and Rascal aged, their teamwork was even better. Rascal still only jumped when prompted, and still never quite caught one of the rodents, but Tommy was getting better at timing.

Tommy was seven when Rascal first caught a gopher. The lab carefully held it in his jaw, and trotted over to the little boy proudly. Tommy, filled with his own pride, went to pat Rascal on the head, when suddenly the dog released the gopher. Tommy squealed and fell back on his bottom as the gopher flailed a moment in the grass before darting away.

Tommy and Rascal had plenty of moments like this together. Gopher chasing was their main source of entertainment in the warmer months. But as it got colder, Tommy's dad would take Rascal out for hours, not coming back until it was nearly dark.

Tommy's parents had explained to him what it was Rascal and his dad did, but all Tommy knew was worry, as he heard the sound of gunfire all day long. It was only when the headlights of his dad's truck lit up the large window of the living room that Tommy felt at ease.

Catching gophers was a task that kept the young boy busy. It kept him out of trouble, made no mess, got him some exercise... really there was absolutely nothing wrong with their playing. They even hauled the gophers far out into the field when they did catch them, in the hopes that the rodents would venture off to a new home.

But this year the gophers were terrible, and Tommy's dad decided it was time to teach his young boy a new lesson. He was ten--he was old enough.

"Tom, come here," he said one afternoon after school. He was standing on the porch, calling to Tommy through the screen door as the boy sat at the dining room table doing homework.

Tommy obediently came, sliding the door shut behind himself cautiously. His dad stood tall, buff with muscle and age, stubble patchy and graying. Tommy enjoyed the look of his dad. He was a rugged man, who could be caring one moment and scary the next.

Right now he had a scary look to him. And he was holding a gun.

"What is it?" Tommy asked, coming to stand beside him, barely passing his dad's elbow in height. Rascal was on his side next to them, basking in the little light left in the day. His ear perked up a tad at Tommy's arrival.

Without a word Tommy's dad handed him the gun, and then proceeded to explain how to hold it. How to fire once the aim was just right. And how it would have quite the recoil when fired.

Once Tommy was in position, confused beyond belief, aiming at a seemingly random spot off in the yard, his dad began to explain. "We're shooting gophers."

"What?" Tommy asked, shocked. After he had finished with homework Tommy was going to go out into the yard with Rascal and scrounge some of them up. Now he was killing them? "Why?"

"They're too big a nuisance this year, Tom. We have to ween 'em down a bit. Ain't gonna cut down the population by having Rascal carry 'em out into the field. They just breed more. So we have to shoot 'em."

Nothing more was said, and the two stood for some time, waiting for a gopher to poke its head up from the ground.

Because there were so many of them this year, it took next to no time at all.

"Right there," his dad said quietly, bending down next to his son and pointing straight ahead. Tommy had seen it--he was practically a gopher-spotting expert. Rascal sat up next to the boy, scooching himself a bit behind Tommy's body, but peeking around at the gopher, as well. "Take your time. When it feels good, shoot."

This would never feel good. That's what Tommy would have liked to say, but the words stuck in his throat. He had the gopher right where he wanted it, could probably hit it on the first try, but...

He'd much rather run around and catch them with Rascal. This just didn't feel right to him.

But with his dad's large hand on his shoulder, he didn't feel like he had much choice. Rascal's warm, big body up against his legs gave Tommy some comfort.

Squeezing an eye shut and biting his lip, Tommy pulled the trigger.

The gun definitely had some kick to it. Rascal helped keep him up, for the most part, but Tommy still ended up jerking back so hard he bounced off the lab and back forward, landing on his bottom. His dad was quick to take the gun from his son's hands before he went to investigate.

Tommy shook. It had been far more powerful than he'd expected. So much so it terrified him. He reached back and patted Rascal's back, thankful for his buddy. Goodness knows he might've gone through the screen door if his dog hadn't been there.

Tommy could see his dad waving to him from about where the gopher was. He couldn't hear a word he said, though, but the small smile on his face indicated Tommy had hit the critter. His dad was still talking as he walked back up to the porch.

But all Tommy had in his ears was the *crack* and *boom* of the gunshot.

20.
Hound Sounds
Terry Sanville

After our boxer Bruno died, his mate Hilda became Dad's constant companion. During the days she slept in his artist studio, strategically camped in front of the glowing space heater. At night, Dad carried her upstairs and laid her on a blanket next to his side of the bed. The vet told us that arthritis had damaged her hips and that she couldn't climb or run anymore.

Nancy had assumed the role of mother to the barn cats and to Fog, our fluffy gray house cat. Carolyn seemed too busy reading her fashion magazines to save much interest for pets. I had tried making friends with some of our neighbors' cows, liking the Holsteins the best. But you couldn't put a cow in your lap and pet it, make it purr or wag its tail. I needed something to love, to talk to about things that Mama and Dad or my sisters wouldn't understand or, more likely, didn't want to hear.

One summer morning, I went with my parents on a road trip to Reading, to check out the flea markets and estate sales. Mama had furnished most of our house with pieces she had purchased at these places. She liked the simple Pennsylvania Dutch antiques and scoured the townships, looking for more things to cram into our home. Dad became an expert at restoring old stuff and adding his own artistic touches. I didn't care that much for antiquing but liked sketching the people and mingling with the crowds.

We pulled up to a large gravel-covered space next to the Weis Market. Pickups and flatbeds loaded with furniture and so-called "collectibles" filled the lot. I considered most of it junk but enjoyed seeing the weird stuff others thought worth selling. As I made my way down the crowded aisle between the rows of vehicles I heard whining coming from the cab of a beat-up GMC loaded with old dressers. I moved quietly and stepped up onto the truck's running board. Inside, a Basset hound stood with his front paws resting on the opposite windowsill.

From first glance, it was obviously a male. He turned his head to look at me with huge sad eyes and gave a perfunctory woof before whipping about and tottering on enormous feet to my open window. His thick tail slapped a steady rhythm against the front seat back. I stretched out a hand and let the dog sniff me. He licked it. His tail-wagging increased its tempo. I scratched him behind his dangling ears, ears twice as long as his face. He made strange whoofling sounds.

"Looks like ya found yourself a friend," someone said from behind me.

I stepped down from the running board and faced a slight man dressed in city clothes. "I heard your dog whining. I didn't mean to bother him."

"He's no more than a pup, the last of the litter. Still misses his Mama."

I brushed my braids away from my face and noticed the strong stench of DOG on my hands, something akin to dirty gym socks combined with poop. He smelled nothing like our boxers. I wrinkled my nose and the man laughed.

"Yeah, Bassets are a stinky bunch. The wife won't let me keep 'em in the house but I've got a nice warm place in the barn. They're not bad ratters, either."

"How do they like cats?" I asked.

"They're smart enough to ignore 'em. This feller couldn't run fast enough to catch one if he wanted to."

The dog started to yip and whine. I climbed back up and rubbed the bridge of his long nose and his solid chest. "Do you have lots of Bassets?" I asked.

"I breed 'em. Why I do it, don't really know. But families seem to like 'em and they're real friendly, makes up for the stink."

"So... so is this one for sale?"

"For the right price, miss. For the right price."

"So what's the right price for an incredibly stinky dog?"

The breeder laughed. "I'll give 'im to ya for fifty bucks. That's a steal for a purebred Basset."

I frowned. "That sounds like a lot. Let me go talk with my parents and I'll be back."

"Don't be gone too long, miss. I'm leavin' in a half-hour or so."

"Please don't leave till you see me again."

The breeder grinned. I hurried back to where I'd left Mama and Dad inspecting some old kerosene lanterns that had been converted to electric lights. But they had moved on. I scanned the crowd, looking for my British Dad wearing his Scottish plaid cap amongst the bald heads and straw hats. I pushed through the clots of people, getting dirty looks from the ladies who came to gossip and rub elbows with their women friends. I finally found them at a truck packed with old milk cans, some of which had been made into stools.

"You've got to come look at what I've found," I told Mama.

"What is it? It's got to be good. You're all red and trembling."

"Oh it's... it's... well just come and look."

"We will when we're finished with–"

"No, you don't understand. The seller is leaving. You've got to come now."

Dad grumbled something but they followed me. We struggled through the crowd. Every few feet Mama got distracted by something and stopped to chat with the vendor, and I'd pull her away. Finally, we neared the truck and I pointed.

Dad snorted. "Old dressers? Really? Those damn things look to be laminated rubbish, nothing solid about them. Why are you so excited about–"

"No silly, it's not the dressers. Come here and look." My voice slipped into its little girl mode, the one I used on Dad when I wanted something. I grabbed his arm and pulled him to the truck's cab. "There he is."

The Basset hound stared down at us from the open window, its tongue hanging out. Mama and Dad stood with their mouths open. Dad started to laugh just as the breeder approached, sizing up my parents.

"Good afternoon, folks. I see your daughter has brought you to see my prize hound."

"Yes, yes, prize hound indeed," Dad said between chuckles.

"Look, Daddy, he's really friendly." I stepped onto the running board and petted the dog; he started making those funny throat sounds again.

"I can see that," Dad said, grinning. "Will you look at those bloody paws and... and those nails?"

"They're bred to hunt small critters in the ground," the breeder said. "Those nails make short work of gophers and such."

"Yes, I'm sure he'd have a ball digging up my garden," Mama cracked. "Do you really want to buy this dog, Margaret? What in God's name for?"

"Daddy has Hilda and Nancy has the cats," I shot back. "I need... need a friend too. I can take care of my own pet."

"Are you able to pay for its food and vet bills?" Mama asked.

I couldn't think of a fast response to that one. Leave it to Mama to bring up the adult issue of cost. "I have a little birthday money left, if that will help."

Dad stepped onto the running board and shouldered me off. The hound nuzzled his jacket, whining and yipping, undoubtedly smelling Hilda on his clothing. The dog lunged forward and licked Dad's face, leaving drool dripping from a cheek.

"My God, that bloomin' thing stinks," Dad said. We'd have to keep him in the barn or the basement."

"All my dogs are in a barn," the breeder chimed in. They're a hardy bunch, take to the snow just fine, even with them stubby legs."

Dad had continued to pet the Basset and I worried that it might get attached to him, just as Hilda and our beloved Bruno had.

"So how much do you want for this thing?" Mama asked.

Well, ma'am, for such a fine specimen, I think sixty dollars would be fair."

"Hey, you told me fifty," I shot back.

"Well, that I did. That I did. I might be persuaded to let go of such a prize for that paltry sum."

I gave the breeder my little girl smile. "If he's such a prize, why is he the last of the litter to be sold?"

Dad puffed up his chest. "Last of the litter you say? It's usually the runts that get sold last."

Dad and I were in fine form as buyers and the years of dickering with venders at flea markets started to pay off.

"I can tell you this, sir; his litter had no runts," the breeder said, indignantly.

"Yes, well, do the topnotch pups usually have two different-colored eyes?" Dad said. "This poor thing looks walleyed if you ask me."

"Some breeders charge more for that."

"So, to sum up," Dad said, drawing in a deep breath, "you want fifty dollars for a stinking, walleyed runt-of-the-litter dog that will probably destroy my wife's garden and harass my old bitch boxer."

"Well… well I might go down to forty-five if—"

"I'll give you thirty-five, cash."

The breeder sighed. "Let's split the difference. Give me forty and it's a deal."

Dad rubbed his chin and frowned. He took out his wallet and checked his money, then looked at me and slowly shook his head. I squeezed my eyes tight so that they teared up, then gave the breeder a mournful look.

"All right, all right. You've got him for thirty-five."

My dad handed over the bills. I climbed onto the running board and petted the dog that voiced his approval of the deal.

"Do you have a piece of rope to use as a leash?" I asked the breeder.

"I might, but it'll cost ya five bucks," he replied.

I shook my head, opened the truck door, scooped up the Basset, and clutched him to me. He felt solid, his tail wagging at a frantic rate. He stretched his head upward and licked my neck. "Come on, let's go home. I already need a bath."

On the way back to our farm, Dad stopped at Johnny Lott's store to stock up on kibble and canned dog food. We decided to house the Basset in the barn, in the pen that Bruno and Hilda used to occupy. The first night, the dog howled until the moon went down. I got up twice to comfort him and he met me with wagging tail and much yipping and jumping.

I had heard hound dogs bark and howl before on neighboring farms. They had a distinctive call that carried for miles. The Basset's howl sounded similar, but it lasted longer. He began with a few quick barks, followed by a howl that started low and rose in pitch. It sounded like some amateur trying to blow a brass horn. I named him "Bugle."

For a week, I tried keeping Bugle in the barn, each night a repeat performance of howling and barking that made Mama really mad. Dad just downed an extra martini after dinner and slept through it all. I felt afraid that I'd be forced to resell the dog at the same flea market where we bought him if he kept it up.

The second week, I moved him inside and into the stone cellar that housed our furnace and water heater. Dad built me a wooden platform from scrap packing crates and I made a snug little nest of old blankets in one corner with his food and water bowls nearby. Bugle stopped howling. But when all of us went to bed, he'd scratch at the cellar door and I had to go downstairs to shush him.

Finally, I left the cellar door open. Sometime after midnight, I heard the clicking of his nails on the stairs and he came into my room. My floorboards shook when he flopped onto the throw rug next to my bed. When I woke in the morning, he'd retreated to the basement and slept soundly in his nest.

"As least he didn't howl or scratch last night," Mama told me at breakfast. "But I heard him go into your room."

I yawned. "Yes, I'm hoping that once he feels at home here, he'll not have to check up on me in the middle of the night. My bedroom rug now stinks of dog."

"Don't worry, I'll air it out today... and it needs a good beating anyway."

But over time, I got used to Bugle's odor. When school started in September, after breakfast I took him outside to do his business in the field then left him on the front covered porch if the weather looked good. After school he'd see me coming home from the bus stop and start baying his welcome. I bought a leash and took him with me on my sketching forays into the rolling country. We spent hours sitting on hillsides with his head laid across my feet; he snoozed while I drew and painted. Bugle snored loudly and dreamed, letting out little yips and barks that sometimes woke him. He became my new painting companion and I wondered if my Grandfather would have liked him, would have drawn detailed portraits of his goofy-looking face.

I fed Bugle once a day, after supper when Hilda had been carried upstairs to sleep. He got his pendulous ears all messy by swiping them through the wet food or dipping them in his water bowl. I used an old clothespin and a soft pad to clip them together behind his head. He protested at first but grew to expect it and didn't start eating until I squared away his ears.

Bugle paid little attention to Hilda and gave the old boxer only an occasional butt sniff. The breeder had been correct: while the Basset would have liked to chase Fog around the house, his first encounter with Nancy's cat involved much hissing and display of fangs and claws. The dog backed off, whined, and retreated to his cellar nest.

As autumn turned into winter, the nighttime became Bugle's domain. He scratched and whined at the kitchen door, wanting to be let out into the darkness. I stumbled out of bed and opened the door. He shot outside, his white-tipped tail disappearing into the night. He ran through the woods and across the top fields and ridgelines, baying the whole time, chasing real and imaginary rabbits or maybe foxes. The sound continued off and on for hours until he scratched at the kitchen door and begged to be let in, to rest his tired feet and legs, and finally sleep.

One night in late February, with crusted snow on the ground, I listened to his bark as he wandered the countryside. It got hoarser and hoarser and slowed, with seconds passing between each call. The sound got no nearer nor farther, just stayed steady, like some kind of canine foghorn.

I slid from bed and pulled on pants and boots, an old coat, scarf and gloves, grabbed my flashlight, and hurried outside. In the clear night, the still air burned my lungs. I headed up the back road toward the ridgeline, moving fast in the ankle-deep whiteness. Near the top of the back hill, Bugle's song grew closer. The feeble racket stopped, replaced by his pitiful whining and strange throat sounds. He lay on his back on a patch of roadbed with no snow, his stubby feet sticking skyward, his ears flapped back against the ground.

"What's wrong, Bugle boy, you wear yourself out?" I crooned. He whined and rolled onto his side, his thick tail slapping the ground.

I picked him up and set him on his feet. Bugle let out a loud yelp, then flopped onto his side. I sat, pulled him into my lap, and inspected his paws. In the flashlight's glare, they looked swollen. I fingered them gently, and he let me do it. Nothing felt broken. I scratched him behind his ears and he snuggled into me, trying to get warm.

My own legs ached from the fast climb. I stared into the black valley, picking out the barn lights on the neighboring farms, the few late night drivers on the State highway, and the far off Appalachian ridgelines backlit by a gibbous moon. The rush of Maiden Creek and the faint lowing of a cow disturbed the stillness. It smelled cold. Bugle let out a whimper. He was so full of the wanderlust, night after night chasing after something that he couldn't quite see or understand. Sitting there in the blackness, I realized that I felt the same way sometimes, and those times came more often. I wanted to go beyond the borders of that valley, beyond Pennsylvania Dutch Country, to someplace else, make friends, fall in love, paint strange places, write poems, read fine literature, and do something important that didn't need my parents' approval nor money from my relatives.

Clutching Bugle to me, I struggled to stand and descended the hill, feeling my way down the snow-covered road. Bugle sighed, content to enjoy the free ride with no pain. After resting several times, I finally reached the house and crept inside. In the darkness, I slipped into the cellar and laid my dog in his nest, his tail beating a hearty approval. I filled a pail with hot water, added a little Epsom salt from Dad's downstairs supply, and soaked Bugle's feet. He nearly licked the skin off my hand for doing that and fell asleep almost immediately after I finished.

In a few days Bugle recovered from his wandering excess. On our painting trips into the hills, I talked to him, outlined ideas for my escape, the exodus I had vowed to undertake years before. He listened to me ramble. My brush strokes covered the white D'Arches sheets with sepia and gold watercolors. The dog sat patiently as my dreams spilled out, of painting safaris to Paris, Shanghai, Tierra Del Fuego, California. Somehow by speaking them out loud to a dear friend, they became more real and gave me hope.

21.
In Memory of My Uncle's Dogs
Mark Hudson

My uncle once had two dogs Hutch and Goulash,
who were like characters from Hieronymus Bosch.
Animated like Tom and Jerry, racing all around,
Goulash was the first to be buried below ground.
Hutch began to slow down as age crept in,
if there was a bed to sleep in, Hutch leapt in.
Then last February, almost one year to this day,
tragedy beset my family, with clouds so gray.
I was hospitalized with bacterial infection,
I was quarantined, I needed medical protection.
Simultaneously, as if things couldn't get worse,
I began to wonder if my family was under a curse.
My construction working uncle, and aunt nurse,
crashed their car into a tree, they couldn't reverse.
They were both injured, including their canine,
bones were broken, I can just hear the dog whine.
Somehow, all three of them survived the crash,
but this summer their dog was gone in a flash.
They put him to sleep; he was on his last legs,
the friendly welcoming tail no longer wags.
When my uncle visited, he seemed a bit sad,
his pet dog was gone, I too felt a bit bad.
Losing a dog is like losing a best friend,
with imaginary friends all you do is pretend.
And now my uncle is having problems with his back,
so I'm going to keep praying to God for Uncle Jack.
He brought my sister and I our first puppy pet,
the fact that he's suffering makes me upset.
Please God, show your mercy, I beg!

If you birthed me with a tail, I'd let it wag!
Because a dog treats a human being as its master,
and God is the one who is the King of the hereafter.
We can learn a lot from our animal's humility,
and how to respect the supernatural trinity.
God may spell dog, if you read it backwards,
but who'd catch that error? Hewlett Packard?

22.
January 14th
Jay Dardes

She gets up from where she was lying,
stretches leisurely,
and walks slowly to the window.
She scans the back yard at length,
looking for any movement,
anything to delight her
like squirrels, deer, chipmunks, turkeys,
even the odd bear.
But there is only snow and ice, unmoving, frozen,
devoid of color.
After long, patient attention
she makes her way back to the place in front of the wood stove
and lies down again,
closes her eyes,
and dreams of summer,
when a Schnauzer can run, chase animals,
and have many things at which to bark.

23.
Lucy
Lisa M. Scuderi-Burkimisher

When Lucy Lu pulls her favorite stuffed fox out of her toy bin and plays with it for hours, I can't help but feel the smile on my face. When she gets a clean bill of health at her yearly checkup, I breathe a sigh of relief and hold her tiny body in my arms. When she's afraid of a thunderstorm and cuddles in my arms, I know she has a sense of security and needs me, as I need her. I know what it's like to be a true mother; a mother who loves her furry baby.

A mother who loves her Shih-Tzu.

24.
My Canine Comforter
A.J. Huffman

Shaking, somewhere inside engulfing folds
of fabric, my Chihuahua cowers. Forecast foretold
long before weather warning beacon beeps,
teletype crosses television screen. The thunder is coming,
so I sit next to quivering lump of satin,
trying to soothe sporadic bursts of physical vibration,
wondering if this is some form of animal Morse Code.
The longer bouts as dashes, short flutters as dots.
His tiny body begs: Mommy, mommy, turn off the rain!

25.
My Canine Friend
Celia P. Ransom

She cocked her head and looked at me
With intelligent eyes, this magnificent Welsh Corgi.
She knew, I swear, that I was sad
For that day lay dead, my Dad.
My heart was breaking o'er such tremendous loss
But she settled next to me and with her paws
Touched my arm in a comforting gesture
A simple canine moment that helped lift the pain, the
Pressure.
And as I stroked her coat again and again
She was what I needed—A quiet but sympathetic
Friend.

26.
My Chihuahua Tries
A.J. Huffman

to comfort me as our nightly hours tick
slowly. He licks my nose to show he approves
of the movie I selected, curls up on the pillow,
paws at the pages of my journal in encouragement
as I write. He even spreads himself out
against my back, becomes a canine heating pad
when I'm uncomfortable, frustrated with the insomnia
that keeps us both from falling into any kind of slumbering peace.

27.
My Literary Lions
Patricia Holland

I've always loved the large lion statues that flank the steps leading up to the main doors of the New York Public Library. If memory serves, the friends-of-the-library members in New York are called Literary Lions.

After I moved to a Kentucky horse farm, I missed those statues—and those friends. Now I only see the lion statuary on my rare visits to New York. However, I do have large dogs that often stretch out on my farmhouse porch, still as statues, calmly, majestically looking out over "their" property. Now I know that the two of them are Literary Lions.

I really should begin with a few details about my farm's odd ball trash service. The trash man comes by once a week. He often reminds me, "There are rules." He won't do driveways---so the trash must be left at the edge of the road down at the end of the farm lane. He'll only pick up three big leaf bags of trash per farm. He's trained his farm clients to call forty-eight hours before trash day if they plan to leave rusty farm implements or old furniture for him to haul away—because on those trash days, he has to bring a helper to load the truck. He won't take more than one piece of furniture per week per client.

Over the years, my neighbors and I have developed some techniques to keep our trash man happy on days when we have a lot of trash. For example, one time when I piled up four bags of trash—not three—I called my neighbor to see if I could give him one of my bags to set out with his trash.

This week, I returned the favor. I got a call from that neighbor. His daughter had just graduated from college with a Bachelor of Arts degree in English. That was the good news. After the graduation ceremony, the neighbor pitched in to help his daughter clean out her student apartment. For some reason, that day they didn't spend any time sorting her things into a keeper pile and a discard pile. They brought everything home with them. He laughed about it over the phone then said, "Now, for the bad news. Most of her old furniture has to go and the discard pile filled up nine big trash bags." The neighbor asked if he could bring over an old bookcase and two bags of trash to put out with mine.

Sometimes, Kentucky's springtime weather is perfect. Trash day this week was one of those wonderful days. It was too nice to stay indoors so I whistled up the dogs and we all moved out on the porch. At first they stretched out calmly, majestically looking out over the farm. Then they heard the rumble of the trash truck.

My oldest dog, Rudy, considers himself to be the farm dog on duty. He jumped to his feet and took off down the lane to make sure the trash truck driver did not cart off anything valuable.

Lately, Rudy has had Woodford in training as another farm dog on duty. So Woodford raced down the lane after Rudy.

Both dogs came trotting home a few minutes later. Each one held something in his mouth. First Rudy, then Woodford, came up on the porch and deposited a book at my feet. When I read the book titles, I knew I had pretty smart dogs. My Literary Lions brought me copies of *Leaves of Grass* by Walt Whitman and *The Poetry of Robert Frost.*

28.
Of Demons and Dogs
John C. Mannone

We found his stiff carcass outside
the woodshed where he had barely dragged
himself, bloated and emptied of light,

except for a hint in the vitreous
of his eyes—a tint of gold
that mirrored streets of his new home.

Mike had some good wolf in him
and he raged against the coming
of the dark. His final hours must have

been wracked in agony, bones dissolving
at the hip. I remember his eyes the days before,
that look of trust in me to bring him peace.

But I am no savior.

Unable to escape the wallowing,
the stench from his own urine,
the defecation smeared on his fur,

he'd howl all night engaging the darkness.
In the morning, his slumped form,
still as death,

baring fangs. His tongue curled
over his teeth lay limp on the ground.
An angel of mercy silenced the pain,

and his demons fled.

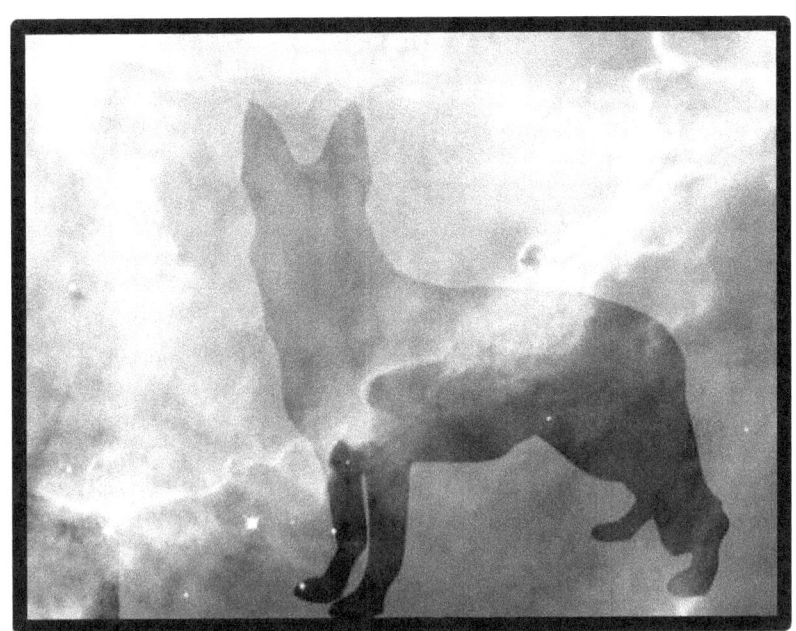

Of Demons and Dogs
John C. Mannone

29.
Of Possums and Poetry
Stephanie Madan

I thought it was my destiny to own Natalie, my neighbor's black standard poodle. If not her, her clone. Natalie is refined. So refined that at boisterous times she must self-medicate by reciting T S Eliot cat poems to herself. This occurs mainly when multiple conversations are initiated by other dogs. I do not judge her any the less superior. Natalie is elegant. I nominate her the Grace Kelly of dogs.

It is my fate to own Amanda, our Westie. This is a dog closely associated with my husband Paul finishing a third glass of Pouilly-Fuissé at a charity event, just as the live-auction puppy was introduced. Amanda is cheerful and self-confident, but any intimations of elegance and refinement are well-concealed.

One night I declined to join Paul at a cocktail party honoring a new automobile model. I am not about to put on a cocktail dress to honor a car. I mocked Paul for being seduced by expensive cars and the prospect of models in miniscule dresses lounging on them. How he found that more appealing than spaghetti casserole and a healthy salad at home is baffling. He ignored my jeers with the air of a man anticipating a pleasant superficial evening with no regret, and so it happened I arrived home alone.

I opened the door. Amanda, poised on the other side, streaked into the garden as I instructed her to sit. My standing as pack leader is one she often ignores, thus neither of us was surprised by this. We were surprised, however, that within seconds she proceeded to corner a possum.

Westies are bred to trap badgers in their dens, providing location-identifying barks until their respective owners arrive. Amanda entered into the spirit of things with ecstatic announcements of her skill that took barking to another level.

Where was Paul when needed? Not answering his phone, that's where. No doubt models were already popping hors d'oeuvres into his mouth while the sales manager assured him he, among all men, deserved to own the first new model in the land. That, as I was confronting Nature.

I called my neighbor James who owns schnauzers and knows things. It was bad luck that James was attending a meeting out of town and that the things he knows are not about possums. He guessed I must wade in and grab Amanda.

First, I was wearing stiletto ankle boots – stylish, but not crafted with actual walking in mind. I am an uncoordinated individual and must concentrate to negotiate a doorway without bouncing off one side or the other. Wearing stiletto boots was more than a fashion statement, it was an act of courage.

Second, it is my highest truth that a two-foot possum transforms into a six-foot hissing monster when trapped by a short, stocky, barking white dog. Amanda remained fearless and engaged full throttle on that barking part even so. I saw the future: She would soon be mauled by a possum that had expected to be staring death in the face and come to realize its situation wasn't remotely dire.

Reader, I saved her. In my stiletto ankle boots I wobbled into the battle, not without encountering rose bushes that wished me ill. I hauled an outraged Amanda out of harm's way, promptly dropped her and managed a body block to prevent her from re-engaging. We retreated to the house where I suffered baleful glares that not even the offering of a raw chicken wing could soften.

There's a moral lurking somewhere. I hate the fact that it may be when in doubt about accepting an invitation to honor a car, just do it.

I suppose something about destiny and poodles would also be appropriate. How will I ever know whether Natalie is my destiny or just my idea of my destiny? Natalie recites poetry. Amanda yodels at possums. I rescue Amanda from monsters. The answer lies in there somewhere.

30.
Porch Guardian
Christopher Woods

The old house as you left it,
the rocker, the door that takes you
into the past, forty, maybe fifty
years ago,
and magically, the old dog,
always the patient friend,
still there,
waiting to greet you,
as if you never left
at all.

31.
Squirrel Spaniel (Cinquain)
Irish Goat

Papillon
sheer delight
licking smiling wagging
brimming with unconditional love
companion

32.
Strolling in the Park
Renee Batenjany

Fritz and Frieda arrogantly promenade slowly to the local park with their German family.

As the noble parents stopped to admire their youngest family member, Rolf Morris was found rolling on his back enjoying the sun rays and the green cool grass in the common garden area.

The twins, Doris and Boris, dashed with a flash to the reserved dog run.

The twins froze with a pause for a cause when they spotted an injured Great Dane with a lame leg and a twisted bruised tail limping with difficulty and crying softly.

Doris barked to alert her parents where they were, then Doris sniffed the injured Dane with the lame and licked his face to let him know he was not alone.

Boris ran with his high innate instinct calling out with a pleading bark to a familiar ranger, urging the ranger to follow him to the injured party.

Ranger Blake gave comfort to the Great Dane. He treated his weepy red eye and twisted tail A call was placed to Doctor Sherman for further assistance.

Ranger Blake was amazed at the twin's quick outstanding and sensitive response. He presented Doris and Boris Doberman with an emblem on a red collar for a splendid and supportive rescue.

Dan released a surprising sweet sound echoing an invite to all his four legged friends in the park to attend a celebration in honor of his rescue by the Doberman twins, thanking them for their kind support during his time of crisis.

The four legged friends were jumping around Dane and his Doberman friends with joy. Many flavors of dog bisques and beef sticks were served to all the guests.

A special dingo treat was passed on to the twins from Dane and all was good and sweet.

33.
Thanksgiving with the Dogs!
Mark Hudson

I spent Thanksgiving with a friend of the family, Carol, because my family is spread out all over the country. Her husband Al, who passed away a long time ago, loved dogs so much that he had one dog he loved, and then he bought another, and they weren't getting along, so he brought them to a dog psychiatrist!

When I came to Carol's house, her son Jay was vacuuming the rug, to get rid of the hairs from his dog, Big Boy. I guess when he used to live with a former roommate he had a dog named Sugar, which supposedly was a contradictory name, because apparently he was a wild, crazy dog! He used to go ballistic whenever he heard vacuuming, so he taught Big Boy how to do the same.

Big Boy really was a big dog! If he lay down on the rug, you weren't getting around him!

There was another person who brought their dog, and in my mind, I'm losing track of who it was. There were two very little dogs and all three dogs competed for attention, chasing each other around the house, and begging to be petted!

They kept begging for Thanksgiving food, and I don't remember if anybody gave them any scraps. Come to think of it, that reminds me that one of the dogs was named Scrappy! And no, he was not named after Scrappy Doo, Scooby Doo's nephew!

Then another lady showed up late, Emily, and she brought her dog, which I don't know what breed it was, but it was just as gigantic as Big Boy! I remember he had a huge tail, what she called a question mark tail!

With all the dogs around, it made things more lively, and I think was probably one of the best Thanksgiving events they had there!

The next day I was supposed to get together with my friend Barbara on Black Friday, and it was raining "cats and dogs" as the cliché goes. I went to the coffee shop across from my house to wait for her to show up, and there were some people from the Thanksgiving dinner in there as well! We were kind of like, "Long time, no see!"

Barb and I went to the Mexican Museum in Pilsen in Chicago, then she took me to a Vegan restaurant because she is such an animal activist she refuses to eat meat. She insisted that everything would be delicious. They take vegetables and make everything taste just as good as meat.

It really was true! I had a Rueben and a cookie dough milkshake and it was all so delicious, and she insisted it was all healthy, and as I left, I did not feel bloated like I might otherwise!

On the way home, a car was in front of us, and the man let a silver-haired lady cross the street with a giant dog. We were shocked to see what could've only been a drunk driver come barreling past us, driving past us, and practically running over the lady and the dog! They looked very frightened. It was not cool. Then we saw ahead that he went through another stoplight! Not being a driver, I probably fail to realize how lucky we were to be alive. Barb being the driver, said, "That hit a little too close to home." But at the same time, there must be a saint who protects dogs and their owners, because thank God that drunk driver did not hit that lady and her dog. I mean I can't prove he was drunk, but the only other explanation would be the cops were chasing him, or he was racing to a store to get some type of Black Friday deal.   At any rate, when I got home, I kind of went to bed early, thankful for all the joy people and dogs brought into my life, and that often times dogs really are man's (and woman's) best friend!

34.
The Anchor
Matt McGee

November, 2015

James read the email six times before he opened the attachment. He knew by the little paper clip symbol in the top left corner that this, like so many others in years gone by, would be yet another of his cousin Andrew's infamous memory bombs.

Andrew was the unofficial family archivist. Every family has one. The keeper of the forgotten, who delights in placing random photos and documents thought long disappeared into the mailboxes of friends and family, the way World War II landmines randomly drift ashore, startling the natives back in time.

James, thru no fault of his own, was a member of the black sheep side of the family. Not that he or his parents had done anything wrong, but in a strict Irish Catholic family it takes far less to get you banished than one might think. James' father shunned gainful employment, convinced his wife to quit her paralegal job, packed up the kids and left a town where the family had over one hundred years of birth, life and death just to strike out for Southern California. There were some in this very Catholic family who felt the move had been the equivalent of having spat in their grandmother's eye. It wasn't the same of course, and their grandmother was long dead, but still, everyone in the family had an opinion about their departure.

It would take James the better part of half an hour to finally open the attachment. He'd read, reread and re-reread Andrew's note:

Found this picture of your Dad. Guessing early 80's and your earliest days in California judging by your Dad's hairline.

The decision to move the family west had been met first with dismissal. Then came the strongest of the Catholic emotions, doubt, which is meant to inspire the true pocket ace in the Catholic hand: guilt. If that's overcome, there will be a brief onslaught of insincere anger followed by resignation.

There had been a big going away party for the family. As night settled in, a bonfire was lit using the last of the winter firewood that would've otherwise been left behind for the next homeowner. James saw the similarity to the ceremonies held by tribes just before a human sacrifice is performed where the innocent are to be tossed into a volcano.

It was here, in the flicker of burning maple his father leaned over and said: "when we get to California, you'll be able to get a dog. I think you boys are old enough now to take care of one."

"Even though we know who'll end up feeding and bathing it and taking it to the vet," James' mother chimed in.

"No you won't," James said certainly. "You'll see."

"Yeah," his brother Keith sneered in support, "you'll see! We'll get the world's greatest dog!"

A lot of things had needed talking over, and his mother and father had discussed the dog idea. The boys weren't enthusiastic about the move - no kid is happy about leaving behind everything they've known, so the dog would be a selling point, an anchor to lend a sense of permanence. *Once we're there, the dog is a symbol of that new life. Care for it the way you would any new life.*

And when James finally opened Andrew's email that rainy afternoon in his small North Hollywood studio, there they were.

His father stood on the back porch of their new home outside L.A., morning sunshine forcing his eyes to squint. He is about the age James is now. Something about his posture hints at exhaustion, but a smile stretches bravely as the California morning shines on his best work clothes. With one hand he grips a steaming coffee mug, and he is using the other to lean down and scratch the ear of the family's new dog. The animal has propped against his thigh, stretching for attention. Her back paws are anchored to the ground. Even in her quest for attention, she never lets go of the earth where they've landed.

April, 1981

In Delaware, bedtime had been the safest place in the world. The embrace wasn't just a favorite blanket or safe, familiar darkness, but the peace a young boy feels at the end of a long day when the world has exhausted him. The quiet of the bedroom would be broken only by the hum of his brother's humidifier whirring in the corner and the occasional burst of his parent's laughter, echoing from the den where the old TV would be tuned to The Carol Burnett Show.

Out west though, the arguing would start early. The new cabinet TV, a splurge for the family, is rarely on. James lay awake, sleep disturbed by the bickering. He could never make out words, but if they threatened his sanctum he'd reach for the clock radio beside his bed and tune in a local AM station.

In the morning he'd emerge to the wreckage; piles of bills scattered across the dining room table, some printed in red, others with receipts stapled to their corners. James would line up a bowl and pour out some Alpha-Bits, minding the finish on the oak wood table and his mother's repeated warnings not to use too much milk.

They owned nothing. James and Keith couldn't play at their previous speed without hearing a shout about touching the walls or abusing the carpet.

"It's a beautiful day outside," his mother would point. "You've got a bike and a nice big field across the street. Go put it to good use."

"When are we going to the pet store?"

His mother would then continue to stir whatever she could afford to fix for dinner, or go on reading a celebrity column in the newspaper. She'd shake her head; these rich and famous people lived within miles of their new home yet she hadn't a single sighting to report back to relatives.

"Ask your father about the pet store."

"I asked yesterday. He said to ask you."

"You know what I think. Ask him again."

So James did what older brothers do: he assigned his younger brother to a routine of nagging and whining. Two weeks later, he and Keith were following their father into a pet store in the mall.

Keith ran ahead of the pack and slammed hands first into the glass enclosures where puppies bounced in beds of shredded newspaper.

For Keith it was like washing up on a shore he'd been paddling toward for months. His original tact had been asking, which after a few days became whining, then the inevitable 'you-promised' bawl. James watched a salesman approach his Dad; the younger guy in polyester vest interlocked his fingers at the waist.

"Something for your sons, sir?"

His dad nodded, but James knew the panicked look. His father had spotted the price tags on the enclosures; jagged red and white explosions with large numbers and small dollar signs were written in magic marker.

"We're just... looking right now," his Dad nodded. James knew the wait and the whining were going to continue. He waited until bedtime that night, keeping himself awake, knowing that twenty minutes after he and Keith's disappearance the voices would rise. When they did, crossed to the bedroom door. He pressed his right cheek into the pile carpet and pushed his ear against the space between the floor and bedroom door.

"We *cannot* afford a pet store dog," his father said sadly.

"For once we agree. But I'm not sure I can afford to keep my sanity if he keeps up that nagging one more day," said his Mom.

"So. What are our options?"

A sheet of newsprint could be heard unfolding. "I'll check the classifieds. People are always giving dogs away."

"People usually give those dogs away for good reason. We don't want some mangy thing that's going to bite the kids and cost us hundreds in doctor bills. Or worse, bite a neighbor and get us sued."

"We're not going to get *sued*."

"We will if you adopt Cujo."

His mother's attention apparently waned; her eyes searched the classified ads. "Have some faith."

"I did. Here we are."

A heavy moment of silence.

"Do you want to leave?"

A heavy sigh. "I don't kn—"

"Don't even *think it!* We've been here seven weeks. Have you been outside? It's January and it's sixty-four degrees during the day. To keep warm at night all we need is one of those Duraflame logs. We're not leaving."

"I didn't say we were leaving. I'm—"

"We're not leaving!"

"Okay," he could hear his father say calmly. "But something we need to talk about..."

"...what..."

"...is the cost of this house."

"It's too much but it's what we could get."

"It's twelve-hundred dollars a month for crying out loud. We can't stay here and get ahead. We have to..."

"...find something. Fine. I'll find something..."

Newsprint rustled again. James turned and sprinted back to bed as if outrunning a monster. Move? Again? No. He'd run away first.

James slept in that morning. Keith, however, had bounced out of bed on time, having slept the sleep of the innocent. James wasn't really awake when he came out his bedroom door, just in time to watch Keith charge in the front door, arms and legs flailing, an excited dog at the end of a leash.

The 'puppy' that led his brother indoors weighed half as much as Keith. With shaggy black coat and thick paws, it began sniffing every inch of real estate. He and James dropped to their knees and rolled on the carpet with the huge, hairy animal while their parents conversed in hushed, clipped tones.

"Oh m'gosh, what is that?"

"She's a Newfoundland."

"She's huge. Oh my... gosh." James had never heard his mother swear. It seemed like she was deliberately trying not to now.

"Granted she's a big one," his father said, "but she's a real sweetheart. And she loves the boys."

"Just don't let her pee on anything and ruin our deposit."

"You hear that boys? If the dog goes inside, you swat her on the fanny with a rolled up newspaper then send her outside."

Their mother raised a brow. "Does she have a name?"

"We were thinking Brandy."

"Brandy? Look at that black fur. What kind of name is that for a black dog?"

"What are we supposed to name her, Onyx?"

"That's not bad."

"Dad!" Keith shouted. "We're gonna take Brandy outside!"

James' father shrugged and looked at his wife. "I think Brandy's gonna take *them* outside."

The three ran loose thru the backyard. When they stopped to pet her, Brandy's fur was thick enough that the boys could burrow in at her thickest spots and still not find skin. As James ran his fingers into her coat, his hands disappearing up to the wrist, he felt himself attached to the dog like nothing else since before the move. Brandy would stand there, rooted, while James latched on. He imagined the rest of his body floating like a Space Shuttle astronaut—but the part that was attached to the dog stayed anchored firmly with the ground.

He and Keith and Brandy ran in circles around the backyard while their father watched from the sliding glass door. James' mother sat at the dining room table; she lifted a folded section of newspaper and continued circling ads in red ink.

Once they'd worn each other out, the dog and boys all plopped down together in their bedroom. Exhaustion settled in early enough to miss the rise of voices, coming from a room nearby.

****

Every morning when breakfast was poured, Brandy gladly accepted whatever dry brand had run a coupon in that week's paper. She'd gallop beside the boys into the field across the street. Sometimes James would suddenly leap from beside the den couch where he'd been peacefully watching TV, sprint through the kitchen, dining room, living room and back to the den, the dog hot on his heels. He'd slide back in front of the TV, and Brandy would stand there like 'what was *that* all about?' Then, slowly, she'd settle beside him again. She'd eventually learn the boy's neurotic tendencies and be content to just sit, watch them run in circles, burn off energy, keeping an eye on them from a warm spot on the rug.

With the passage of weeks and months, the reasons to stay in California were becoming fewer and fewer. Finances continued sliding backward; his father's new job paid only a little more than what he'd made in Delaware, and they couldn't live on that. His father continued to go to work while his mother continued circling rental ads in the newspaper.

Then, just weeks before their cash and credit were due to run out, along came the house. A four bedroom ranch home on five acres of hillside property owned by a former famous western actor. Only $500 a month. They called. They got the place in the hills.

The boys learned to live with the threat of scorpions, coyotes, and a half dozen other very real predators, including an old man named Christy who would drive his Dodge onto the property and park beside the house just to watch the sunset. Christy initially said he was a former resident, then claimed to be a realtor looking to selling the property. James' father called the number on the card Christy had produced; the manager claimed to know nothing about the guy. During his next unannounced visit, James' father not so politely invited Christy to keep himself and his car at the end of the long driveway from then on. Christy showed once more, and when James met him at the gate with a crescent wrench hung dangerously in one hand, Christy drove off.

Brandy, of course, took to the hills like one of the jackrabbits. She'd outgrown her leash, and the boys hadn't gained enough weight to harness her. Suddenly turned loose, Brandy bounded through the brush; it was their mother who eventually demanded the dog wear a collar.

"If she goes missing, if she gets away from you kids someone will need to know who to call to get her back home." Everyone agreed this was sound advice and from then on the dog could always be heard coming, tags 'a jingling. The threesome would run into the hills, exploring until the sun weakened, then they'd sprint back up the hill toward the ranch house.

Now along with booming Delaware thunderstorms and shouting voices, James could add the sound of yipping coyotes outside his window to the list of things that had carried him to sleep. Brandy would stand up and bark back, not out of some primal sense of longing but the way a burglar alarm alerts owners to a danger just outside their door. Eventually the wild dogs would settle, and Brandy would curl back up at the foot of the boys' beds, but her eyes were slow to shut.

James started school in a new junior high that had been built only a few years earlier. He'd discover girls, the thrill of passing notes in hallways and of competing in the sports he'd always been good at. And when the school day ended he'd come home, romp with Brandy and start playing video games. The time seemed one of peace and healing, when the bills were being caught up on, the ship was righting itself, and for once, the sailing had become smooth.

Then came the Tuesday afternoon when James walked up the steep hill and, coming to the foot of the driveway, saw the four police cars scattered across their yard. He dropped his books beside the mailbox and took off in a sprint.

"What's going on," he demanded of the first cop he came to.

"Do you live here?"

"Yes. What's—"

James saw the Dodge parked in the side yard.

"What's that guy doing here," James demanded. "Why's his car back in our yard?"

James didn't even wait for an answer; he pushed forward and went right toward the garage, knowing where he'd left his wrench. If he saw Christy -

"Whoa there, fella." The cop moved to block James. "Why don't you tell me who this guy is."

James opened his mouth to tell about the guy who'd creep around the house, park in their yard and come back after being told not to. He'd just opened his mouth when Keith came running from the house.

"James!!" Keith ran right at his chest and gripped on.

"What's going on with all the cops?"

"That guy came in the house. Brandy went after him. Then she ran off in the hills!"

James looked up to see Christy coming at them. "That damn dog bit me! So help me I'll have it caught and put in the pound. I'll sue your parents for every last penny they've got and—"

"STAY OUT OF OUR HOUSE!!" Keith yelled.

"Did you walk in the house sir?" said one of the younger cops.

"That dog ran right up and bit me! I'll—"

"Did you walk in the house sir?" the cop repeated.

"He turned the doorknob and opened it and Brandy went right at him. She never bit him! He hit his hand on the doorjamb, once Brandy came up and scared him. He was all swinging around like he was going to hit her, and she took off. Into the hills."

James noted the mellowing sun. "We need to find her."

"She'll come home," one of the cops said. "Dogs are smart."

"She's probably scared," Keith said. "She won't come back so long as this jerk is here."

Christy was about to say something when their mother's blue Chevy appeared at the foot of the driveway. She stopped, got out and came right at the whole group. Christy seemed to shrink back a step, toward the house, his car.

"What's going on?"

James had never seen or heard his mother worried. The officers began to give her the story. A few sentences in she interrupted with "are my boys in any kind of trouble?"

"No, ma'am."

"Boys," she pointed, "go find Brandy. I'll handle this."

"They're witnesses!" Christy pointed. "I'll file suit in court first thing Monday for—"

The last thing James heard as he ran out of earshot was his mother rattling off a list of charges learned as a paralegal: criminal trespass, intimidation, breaking and entering, assaulting a minor.

James passed the house, into the five hilly acres of dry brush and coyote trails. He knew Brandy's favorite routes and tracked her like an Indian. Their acreage was bound by only a barbed wire fence, which then led into the famous western actor's property. There was a set of servant's homes, and eventually, endless acres of open land. His brother was a good hundred feet ahead of him, shouting Brandy's name, giving her favorite whistle, whatever might bring her back. Eventually, James caught up to him.

"I swear," Keith said, "if that guy got Brandy killed I'm gonna kill him right back."

James squinted into the sun. It was setting faster than he thought it could. "We should head home."

"We haven't found Brandy yet!"

"She'll come home. The cops said so. Besides, coyotes come out at night. C'mon."

"But we have to *find* her!"

James started toward the house on top of the hill. "C'mon. She'll know what to do."

His brother continued to yell but eventually followed him up the hill. When they got back to the house it was almost dark. Their father was there. Christy was leaned against a police car, his wrists bound with shining cuffs like the kind they'd seen on *Hill Street Blues*. When their mother looked their way, she seemed to mostly be looking for the dog. And when she saw she wasn't there, she leaned her head sympathetically. Then she looked away, into a distance that seemed to point north, toward the place they'd come so far to escape.

That night there were no coyote howls, though James waited up to hear them. It was as if they were too busy to bother, or had moved off somewhere further away, somewhere familiar.

And in the other room, James heard the voices again. He couldn't make out their words as usual, but he knew the tone wasn't one of two adults arguing. His mother must have been passing his door when she said:

"It's just too much."

James turned on the AM radio. They weren't hammering out a compromise, debating coupons or weekly specials; instead, they spoke in hushed tones of resignation. And he knew, as he lay in the dark, an empty dog blanket at the foot of his bed, they'd all be going home soon.

35.
The Joy of Walking
Betty Hartnet

"God made human beings so dogs would have companions."
~Frederick Seidel, an American poet

The Cardinal's flash of brilliant red,
The pale outline of the moon still visible,
The Crow perched on top of the tallest tree,
The delicate flight-song of the American Goldfinch,
The sparkling of silver poplar leaves,
The rows of pine and spruce,
Shadows that grow, bend, and shrink,
The yellow of dandelions,
The sweet aroma of the lilacs,
The azure blue of the sky,
The endless variety of cloud formations,
Spunky squirrels and cautious rabbits.

The joy of walking
I learned from my dog.
We set out,
his nose searching for smells,
my eyes reaching toward nature's splendor.
Gratitude flows.
We walk in joy.

36.
The Leash
Lynne Adams

The leash was frayed in several places.   The sheen had long ago left the woven nylon strip, giving way to a comfortable fuzziness around the edges.

Dried mud clung to its edges; dusty grime shadowed its length.   The loop of the handle was a well-worn curve perfectly sized to slide over a hand holding a ball.

She draped the leash over the hook by the door, letting its tired coils unfurl to the floor, a metallic clink echoing in the house as the clasp hit the tiles of the entrance hallway.   Broken bits of curled-up leaves settled under the ends of it, and for once she didn't mind them.

The leash sat on the "Good Dog" hook, an engraved image of a smiling dog atop it.   Next to it was the "Bad Dog" hook, with the exact same dog smiling away in blessed contentment, oblivious to the notion of 'Good' and 'Bad'.

She gently held Duke's collar, a thick leather slab with burnished metal studs imbedded in it and the sweet stench of a dog's life buried even deeper in its grain.   The tarnished name-tag, obligatory city license, and vet- encoded I.D. hanging from the metal buckle all tinkled together as she lifted the collar and set it in its place, canine chimes filling the empty space in her heart, for a moment, erasing the aching absence in the house.

Duke was now forever a Good Dog.

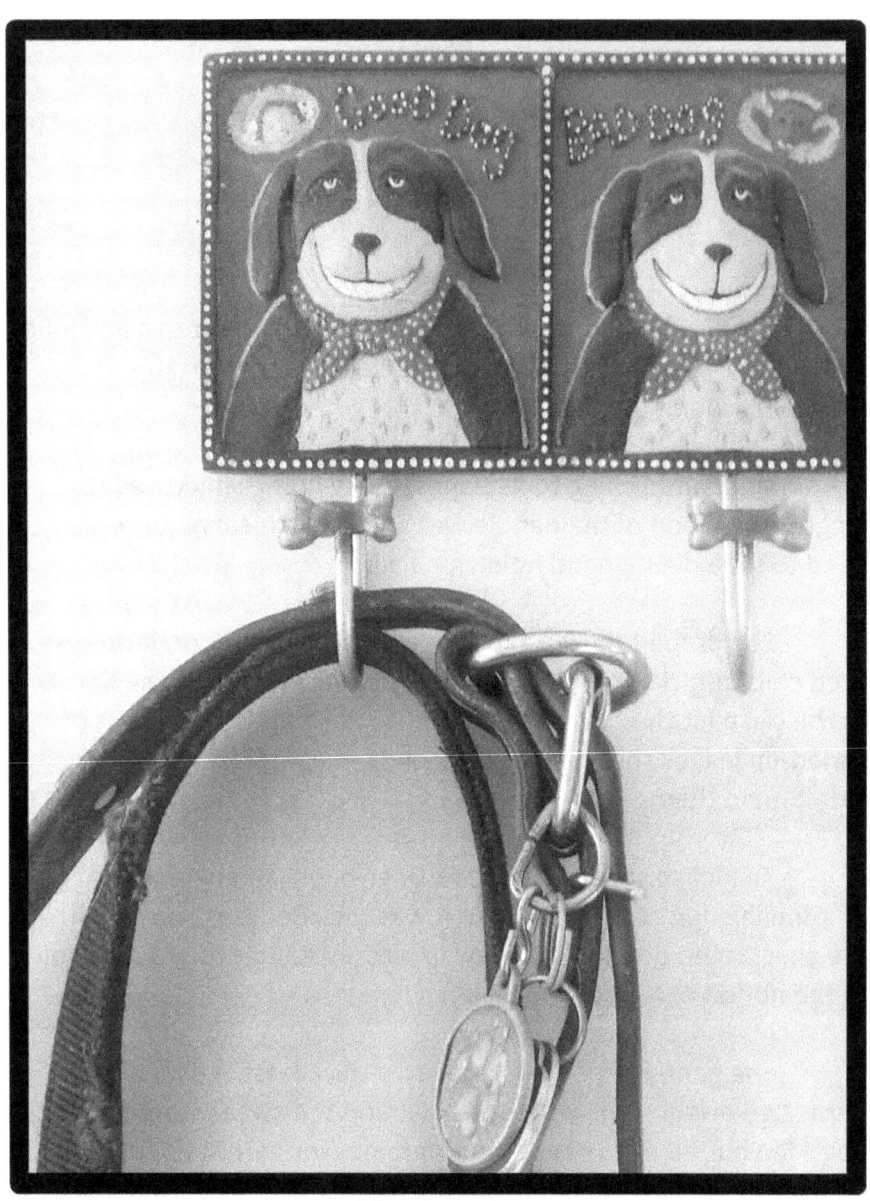

The Leash
Lynne Adams

37.
A Story of Hope:
Just an Old Farm Dog
Patricia Holland

The miserable-looking dog limped across our farm yard. At first glance, that was all I saw. Her ribs stood out, easily counted. She hadn't been fed in a long time.

Mangy? Yes, she was that, too. She had rubbed all the hair off her tail and scratched most of the hair off several other spots. Her teats swung and moved with every step. Wasn't that a sign that she had recently had puppies? No sign of the puppies now, just a lost mother dog in need of some human kindness.

I opened my door.

Later, I learned more of her story. I discovered that she had never experienced human kindness---only hurt had come from the humans she knew. Right from the time they got her as a puppy, her owners kept her locked in a small, fenced yard with a set of scrappy, fighting dogs. Within a year she became pregnant. Her owners chained her to a tree just outside of their yard. Sometimes they fed her and provided water. Sometimes they did not.

When her puppies came along, they were weaned and immediately taken away from her and sold. That happened over and over again.

When her owners were evicted, they sold off their fighting dogs, but they made no provisions for the old mother dog. They never cared or considered how the sun would beat down mercilessly on the dog they left behind, shackled on a short chain, left without food or water.

To survive, the dog slowly chewed through the metal chain, breaking several teeth in the process. Making her way into town, she approached several people. Some simply shooed her off their doorsteps. Others kicked her away.

She camped out near the campus McDonald's for several weeks after she discovered that college kids would throw some of their fries and leftover burgers her way. One day, while zooming away from the carry-out window one of them had hit her with his car.

Then one day she limped out of town and found our farmhouse. Despite all the bad things humans had done to her, when I opened my door and approached her for the first time, she wagged her tail. At the first touch of my hand, she raised her eyes and looked up at me with hope and unfailing love.

To me, it looked like she was thinking, "I hope you take me into your home. I hope you'll feed me. I hope you'll let me stay." So I named her Hope.

Within a few days, Hope had favorites: a favorite sunny spot in the farmhouse kitchen, a favorite blanket to nap on, and a favorite kitten to lick and love like a puppy. Watching the dog explore her new home and accept all the love her new "family" lavished on her reminded me of the following line from an old hymn: "Hearts unfold like flowers before thee, opening to the sun above." The melody of that hymn is from the Ode to Joy a theme in "Beethoven's Ninth Symphony, but the words and name of the hymn tune came later when it was named the "Hymn to Joy."

Years have passed since the day I found Hope—and she found her forever home. Each day that old farm dog has returned love a hundredfold. She's become a self-appointed helper around the place. She has adopted orphan lambs and helped to raise them. She has been my companion especially when I work in the garden. Afterward, she has always enjoyed an ice cube slipped into her water bowl, slurping it up as I sit nearby companionably sipping my iced tea.

The backseat of my car is her throne during our trips to town. Yes, she always earns a burger at McDonald's while we're there (however, we've both cut out the fries). As I drive, if I begin humming the music to the "Hymn to Joy," the dog cocks her ears and seems to be listening.

Back home on the farm, she may tear out of the car when she spots a deer or a rabbit, but she always slows down before she catches them. I gather she just enjoys the chase. Whistling a few bars of Beethoven's music from the "Hymn to Joy" always brings her back out of the woods.

Each Christmas, she has remained unfazed by a blizzard of wrapping paper, noisy toys, and noisier grandchildren who are apt to hang all of their ribbons around her neck. Even wreathed with bright ribbons, there is no way to make her a pretty dog. She's just an old farm dog, but to me she is lovely. With or without the ribbons, she's God's gift to me—a shining example of trust, joy and love.

38.
The Pack
(Nonet, Progressive, Reverse)
Irish Goat

Wolves
hunt
in packs.
They
seem to
understand
that
culture
and the life
of each member,
the
entire
party, is
interwoven.
Every wolfling
plays
its part.
The pup is
encouraged to
adhere to mores,
the pack experience.
This
ensures
collective
acceptance to
traditional laws.
To understand also
establishes culpable

acts.
Justice
is meted,
the penalty
severe. Every
issue answerable,
according to tradition.
Usually, they are exiled.
Our
culture
has often
rejected the
scientific fact:
man is a predator.
We claim civilization
has proven our evolution.
We institutionalized the pack.

39.
Warmth (Sedoka, Triple)
Irish Goat

I expected warmth,
but as we left the shelter,
all of your smiles disappeared.

I expected warmth,
but you simply ignored me.
I was the translucent one.

I expected warmth,
but was tethered to a spike,
you gave no shelter or shade.

I expected warmth,
but no doors opened to me.
I wear thin skin, snow and rain.

I expected warmth,
but your world was cold to me.
Warmth can be lost from a heart.

I needed that warmth,
but have new expectations:
Death now ushers in freedom.

...and warmth.

40.
Where's The Beef?
Stephanie Madan

I apologize for that recent excitement at Puerto Vallarta International Airport. Although it has never been my ambition to create an international incident, there are some things you just have to do. Someone had to speak for the dogs.

Amanda, our Westie, and Rachel, our sort-of wire hair terrier, joined us on that trip to Puerto Vallarta. It was Rachel's first visit to our house there. They were both arriving via automobile the following day, escorted by a colleague of ours they seem to love more than us. In any case, Rachel was enjoying an extended puppyhood and felt it her duty to gnaw on anything she could get her teeth into. My husband Paul and I noticed she preferred furniture legs and millwork along the lower edge of walls, but she was not above chomping on those fake plastic tea-light candles set around our pool occasionally to dazzle visitors. An innovative and humane strategy of redirection was called for.

So, I brought chewies with me. Not innovative, true, but unquestionably humane. Rachel enters her state of purest joy when provided with a chewy. She instantly abandons furniture legs, millwork, and plastic faux candles. She jumps into the air quivering with anticipation and executes a double pirouette before she lands; all the while making little squeaks I interpret as endearments meant for the chewy. Amanda, older, considers it deeply uncool to leap for chewies, but she chews on them with enthusiasm, if only for old times' sake.

The chewies I purchased were beef flavored. They were made from a vegetable base so their appeal was solely the flavor of beef. I emphasize that they were beef *flavored* and also in their original packaging. I was not bringing in meaty soup bones, for heaven's sake.

I define food as a substance one voluntarily places in one's mouth and swallows. Chewing gum, therefore, is not food. Dog chewies, therefore, are not food. They are stand-ins for food. Neither is swallowed. If the general population has accepted that chewing gum is nowhere to be found in the food pyramid and if dogs everywhere have determined the same thing regarding chewies, what prevents the crack team of customs agents managing import security at Puerto Vallarta International Airport from doing so?

This is how import security is managed by the customs office at Puerto Vallarta International Airport: Press a button – If the light is green, you may continue your journey. If the light is red, you are not going anywhere till the person in charge says so. This is putting a lot of faith in a button. Seriously, how many threats to Mexico's well-being have been neutralized via this method? Well, now we know of at least one.

Paul and I caught the customs' red light that trip which meant a luggage search before going on our way. We knew the drill. I, for one, was cheerful about it. It gave me an opportunity to pretend I am flexible and not easily ruffled. This matters because Paul has mentioned more than once that he knows of fifteen people he would rather travel with.

We slung our luggage up on an inspection table. A young fellow unzipped my suitcase and noticed the bags of chewies right off. He was stunned by such luck. He had just prevented criminal entry of numerous prohibited items into Mexico.

He eyed me. He looked again at the chewies and continued his inspection with new vigor. This could be a career maker: A genuine incident was unfolding at his table. When you are at the bottom of the customs food chain, thwarting an international smuggler is no small thing. The thrill in his expression was truly touching. Sure enough, there were more chewy bags stuffed in whatever air pockets had been available in my suitcase. He told me they were forbidden. I told him that was ridiculous.

The young man laid the chewy bags out on the table and summoned the customs supervisor of the Puerto Vallarta International Airport.

As I have mentioned, there are times when you have to do what you have to do, no matter that it plays out as an international incident. The battle with the customs supervisor began.

She immediately announced to me in broken English and with finality: The chewies are beef. They are forbidden food. We are taking them.

Her expression was disdainful as she prepared to collect them and be off.

And welcome to you, too. Have some bottled water. Obviously she was making her decision before collecting all the facts so I began to acquaint her with them.

No, they aren't forbidden, I conveyed to her in my inventive Spanish. First, they aren't food. Dogs don't eat chewies. If they did, chewies would not be called chewies. 'Swallowies' doesn't resonate as a replacement, but it would not be difficult to come up with something catchy. In any event, chewies would not be their name. Dogs chew them till the flavors are exhausted and then store them in peculiar places. They do not ingest them. Second, the chewies in question are vegetable based. They are beef-flavored, not beef.

I reached over to pick a chewy bag up to point out the ingredients listed on the label, but that customs supervisor of the Puerto Vallarta International Airport came this close to hammer-locking me to interrupt the process. I was not allowed to touch the contraband even if it was my contraband. I wondered, based on my masterful interpretation of body language, if there was some concern I might swallow the evidence. Ha! My point exactly – the swallowing part. I fell back on Plan B and invited her to read for herself the words on the wrapper. The invitation was declined.

Maybe she had lost her reading glasses, but I suspect she just felt like asserting her sweeping power over me. By now a small crowd had formed, comprised of all the people the young fellow on the lowest rung of the customs food chain could muster. The customs office had an incident going and it was his.

The true nature of the Puerto Vallarta International Airport customs supervisor was revealed as I continued to debate with her. I regret to report she is a sour person. She insisted that the vegetable-based chewy was beef each time I voiced my assertion it was not. She did this in a strident voice of increasing volume. The volume part was pure theatrics, considering we were now in each other's face. Possibly she was concerned the chewies were freeze-dried cows that would rise up as porterhouse steaks with malicious intent once hydrated. At last, I concluded I was communicating with the wrong level of management.

I politely asked to speak to the customs supervisor; thinking a bit of levity might improve the atmosphere. As she did not respond in a light-hearted way, I am guessing my Spanish version of that request was imperfect. Instead I was awarded a glare she did not discard as our dialogue continued.

I was becoming impatient. Willful obtuseness affects me that way. I commented to no one in particular that any person possessing a brain knows vegetable-based dog chewies in original packaging pose no threat to the great country of Mexico. She accepted this in the spirit it was conveyed. Her glare grew fiercer. I was taking less and less pleasure in her company. Plus accusations of smuggling hurt my feelings. I returned her glare.

The customs supervisor began scribbling something on an official-looking form which she eventually thrust into my hands. I asked her if it included the name of her supervisor so I could report her ghastly manners and defective judgment.

There is no one else, she hissed. She was power-mad.

As she scribbled, Paul had edged away from me. Someone needed to remain free to hire the attorney after they took me into custody. For all we knew, that piece of paper consigned me to a dank and squalid Mexican prison. (Charming prisons may exist all over Mexico, but I'm going with the rumors.)

I paused. I saw myself in prison, attired in an orange prison jumpsuit. Orange does not flatter me. Internet access would be absent. Cocktail hour would be absent. Sushi would be absent.

My love for Amanda and Rachel is deep, but rational: Serving a stint in prison would deprive them of a mother and me of almost everything. I hated doing it, but I began a dignified retreat. The supervisor seized the chewies and probably chewed on them herself, at home. It was painful. I was beaten. But I was free.

So, here's how things ended up: Paul and I got to our car and, once safely off airport premises, I deciphered her scribbles. The words announced the items had been confiscated. Nothing more. Next, we stopped by a grocery store on the way to the house. There we discovered Mexican dog chewies on the pet aisle. The pet aisle is one I had never investigated. The chewies we spotted were similar to the ones confiscated. In fact, they were so similar the dogs would not be able to tell. I wish I had known that.

I have since familiarized myself with the prohibited items list. Fruits are prohibited. What about that peach-flavored lip gloss I brought into Mexico? Was the Mexican agricultural system compromised as a result of the flavoring in my gloss? This is a slippery slope that Mexico must face squarely and at once. The threat of peach-flavored gloss has been overlooked. What else has been missed?

When the Mexican government heeds my warning and gets moving on this, everyone in the customs office food chain at Puerto Vallarta International Airport will no doubt be instructed to read the labeling. And if the wise heads of the Mexican government decree that the customs supervisor of the Puerto Vallarta Airport is to be punished by having to wear an orange prison jumpsuit and enjoy no internet access for a month as penance for being so disagreeable, my hurt feelings will be mollified. I have hope, but I manage my expectations.

41.
Woodford's Big Game
Patricia Holland

Woodford, my brightest and best Labrador, has a deep hatred for the squirrels on my farm. Last fall, he patrolled my farm lane warning off the squirrels who tried to "steal" the walnuts that had fallen on the lane. Since the squirrels could move faster than he could, they often succeeded in their goal—to grab the walnuts and run.

So Woodford began training the younger farm dogs—two brainless part Labs—to chase squirrels. Those dogs, Buddy and Gary, look like twins, but I can always tell them apart because Buddy jumps and Gary barks.

Over the winter months, most of the squirrels holed up in hollow trees. They probably spent their days feasting on walnuts. However, one big red squirrel developed a taste for birdseed. As soon as I filled the bird feeder, the squirrel would shimmy down a tree, jump onto the top edge of the fence and scamper over to the feeder. It could eat birdseed faster than a whole flock of birds. I named it Hog. I was determined to go on the offense, to find a squirrel-proof bird feeder, to beat the squirrel at its own game.

I found a beaut of a squirrel-proof feeder. It had a built-in tray covered by a sliding bar with a row of small holes in it. Gravity carried the seeds down into the tray. It was designed so that light-weight birds could stand on the bar and peck out the seeds through the small holes. But as soon as a heavy squirrel tried to stand on the bar, it slid closed covering the holes disappointing the squirrel who quickly learned that no open holes left him with no way to grab the seeds.

When a blizzard brought down twenty inches of snow, Hog the squirrel became a beggar. He would stand under the bird feeder hoping the birds would drop some of their food. I relented and bought him a squirrel feeder—and set it up on the farm gate, far away from the birds' feeder. He loved the new feeder and began hanging around the gate for hours every day. He knew he was safe from Woodford because the dog sank in the snow, but the squirrel could scamper across the drifts to escape.

Spring days finally arrived in mid-March. Yesterday Hog, the beggar squirrel, was back looking for food under the bird feeder. Hog must have thought that Woodford had slowed down during the winter because the squirrel remained under the feeder and watched as Woodford approached with his team.

They acted like an undefeated basketball team racing down-court trying to steal the ball! Like an excellent power forward, Woodford positioned himself between the feeder and the tree line so Hog could not run his usual escape route. It spun away and ran back toward my oldest dog, Ella, the shortest player on the team. She might be short, but she understands the Game of Squirrels.

So the squirrel changed direction again and tried to climb to the top of the fence. Blocked! Young Buddy made his move, jumping high enough to pull Hog back down to the ground. Perhaps in another life, Buddy was a championship college basketball player, probably the center of his team because he was so tall and able to jump.

Unfortunately, Hog charged Gary, the only true freshman player on the farm dog team. He didn't understand the rules of the game. So he stood still, barking but not moving when the squirrel ran right past him.

The squirrel came up the farm lane and dived under my car.

At last Woodford and the other dogs had the squirrel trapped. They must have thought getting it out from under the car would be a slam dunk. They were wrong.

The squirrel found a small hole in the wheel well and got into the space between it and the back bumper. None of the dogs could fit through that hole—but not for lack of trying. After the first dog put a long scratch down the bumper, I joined their efforts to dislodge the squirrel. We had no luck.

I grabbed my car keys and headed for town. When I drove off the farm, the squirrel cussed and clucked all the way. The dogs escorted me down the farm lane and out onto the road trying to catch up to my car. One-by-one as I out-distanced them, the dogs stopped running. Then they put their heads down and slowly headed back up the lane—defeated in their championship game.

There is a happy ending to my story. It only took three mechanics an hour to take off the bumper and send the squirrel racing out of the garage. 'Ere it ran out of sight, a mechanic called out, "Welcome to town little buddy, you're not down on the farm anymore."

42.
You Mean More than the Vastness of the Sky
Norbert Gora

Strong arms of wind
scour your thick fur,
on a hill I can feel the scent
of summer, whispers of easiness.

Your whiteness emphasizes
the purity of my world,
the bliss that spreads inside the heart.

Your look is like therapeutic coat,
with every wink there is more light
in my soul, volcano created with nerves
loses malicious call.

Our two hearts are something more
than letters that make up friendship,
it is a community of unimaginable love
and jumping through the fire
in moments of crisis.

It is two legs and four paws
ready for long journeys,
where the danger has many faces
like the devil.

You mean more than the vastness of the sky,
we are two galaxies in one space.

43.
You Prefer People
Betty Hartnett

It's true that people and pets eventually
resemble each other in appearance or mannerisms
though differences persist.

I'm talking about you and me, Chico. I don't use
my tongue to lick my nose as you are doing

at this moment
and I don't keep my nose to the ground

as we take our daily walks.
Too, I don't like my stomach rubbed

really, I don't.
And I've never chased a squirrel.

But I do love to hike the park trails.
I like treats almost as much as you

and enjoy lying in the summer shade.
Plus, I like people and dogs

same as you, though
you prefer people.

Contributing Authors

Bear

A.J. Huffman

     A.J. Huffman has published twelve solo chapbooks and one joint chapbook through various small presses. Her new poetry collections, *Another Blood Jet* (Eldritch Press), *A Few Bullets Short of Home* (mgv2>publishing), *Butchery of the Innocent* (Scars Publications), *Degeneration* (Pink Girl Ink) and *A Bizarre Burning of Bees* (Transcendent Zero Press) are now available from their respective publishers and amazon.com. She is a four-time Pushcart Prize nominee, a two-time Best of Net nominee, and has published over 2400 poems in various national and international journals, including *Lableter, The James Dickey Review, Bone Orchard, EgoPHobia,* and *Kritya*. She is also the founding editor of Kind of a Hurricane Press. ***www.kindofahurricanepress.com.***

Briana J. Weiss

Briana J. Weiss is a recent graduate from university and a Midwestern homebody. She's loved reading and writing for as long as she can remember, and hopes to one day write her own fiction novel. Her past experience includes being an editor/Editor-in-chief of her university's literary magazine *Prairie Winds*, and earning first place in the Agnes Hyde Writing Competition for poetry.

Celia P. Ransom

Celia P. Ransom is from a small town in Michigan. She has always written. For many years, she simply wrote letters to family and Friends. Around 2005, she began writing poems for friends and her grandchildren. She went through a low point in her life and the writing was a distraction. It took a while; however, to share with others were not close to her. Celia keeps a pen and paper by the bed, as she often awakes in the night with lines of a poem or story going through her head. She has to write it down before returning to rest. When she isn't writing, Celia enjoys reading, well-written and well-acted movies; and speeding time with her family and friends at their cottage in northern Michigan. She also loves chatting on the phone with those close to her. As a child, Celia wanted to be in the movies; although when she thinks about it now, she would probably be terrified.

Celia published a collection of Poetry in 2014; *Poetry Plain & Simple* and has been a contributor to many Grey Wolfe Publishing anthologies, including *Write To Woof 2015; Encore Writers; and The Grey Wolfe Storybook 2014*. ***www.GreyWolfePublishing.com***

Irish Goat

Chris 'Irish Goat' Knodel is an author, poet and ultra-distance runner in San Antonio, Texas. He is a graduate student in the Creative Writing MFA program at Houston University-Victoria. His poetry and short fiction have been featured in/by *Ealain, Haiku Journal, Highfield Press, Kind of a Hurricane Press, The Wolfian, The Write Place at the Write Time, Writer's Quibble, Yellow Chair Review, Zimbell House Publishing, The Zodiac Review & Zombie Logic Review*. He can be easily spotted by his kilt, tattoos and six inch, flaming-red, Van Dyke goatee.

Mark Hudson

Mark Hudson is an author who spends of time reading, writing, and doing art. He recently read of someone who likes to get up early and write, like a lot of writers, and he has found that his best ideas come to him early with really strong coffee. He gets published periodically in different print magazines and on-line, but finds Grey Wolfe has published more of his pieces than anyone else. Mark has relatives in Michigan, and one time he was reading one of the stories in one of the anthologies about an author reflecting on a Michigan childhood, camping, picnicking, inviting friends over to join in hot dogs with families, etc. Mark was almost jealous at how kind everyone seemed in the Michigan story. He told his aunt and uncle this this weekend, and his aunt said, "Yes, that was how my childhood was in Michigan."

Mark is a prolific writer and has been a frequent contributor to *Legends, The Grey Wolfe Storybook, Write To Woof, Write To Meow* and other Grey Wolfe Publishing anthologies. He is currently working on a collection of short stories.
www.GreyWolfePublishing.com

Norbert Gorra

Norbert Gora I'm Twenty-five-year old poet and writer from Poland. Many of my horror and science fiction short stories have been previously published. I'm also the author of the poem *The Feathery Immensity of Blue*, which was a part of English-language anthology of poems and short stories – *Contemporary Writers of Poland*.

John C. Mannone

John C. Mannone has over 500 works published in venues such as *Inscape Literary Journal,* Windhover, Artemis, 2016 *Texas Poetry Calendar, Southern Poetry Anthology (NC), Still: The Journal, Town Creek Poetry,* Tupelo Press, *Baltimore Review, Pedestal* and others. *Author of two literary poetry collections—Apocalypse* (Alban Lake Publishing, July 2015) *and Disabled Monsters* (The Linnet's Wings Press, Dec 2015)—he's the poetry editor for *Silver Blade* and the Hugo-nominated *Abyss & Apex. In 2013,* he was the Rhysling Poetry Chair for the Science Fiction Poetry Association. He won the 2015 Joy Margrave award for creative nonfiction as well as the 2015 Tennessee Mountain Writers poetry contest. He's been nominated three times for the Pushcart Prize. He serves as the Director of Programs for the Chattanooga Writers' Guild, as well as a member of the Knoxville Writers' Guild and the Roane Writers Group. He is a professor of physics in east Tennessee. Visit The Art of Poetry: *http://jcmannone.wordpress.com*

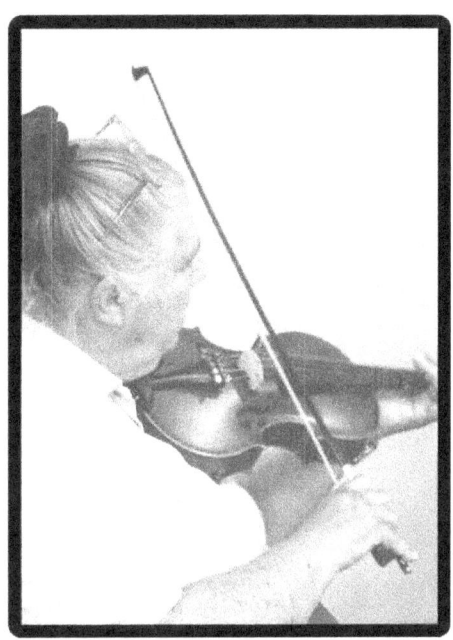

Patricia Holland

Kentucky farmer and freelance writer Patricia Holland is currently working on her first novel. When she was seventeen, she went to work as a proofreader for the National Geographic Society. "I needed money for college plus $300 to buy a hippy van," she says. "I had planned to work for one year then quit to attend college full time, but I liked working for the Society too much to quit; I worked there for more than twenty-five years. P.S. I still own a VW camping van. It has lots of room for my camping gear and my dogs.

Renee Batenjany

Renee grew up in Detroit, Michigan. She moved with her family to Beverly Hills, Michigan and is now living a pleasant walk from Birmingham, Michigan.

Her writing is inspired by others; my feelings and emotions. Renee writes Thank You notes for Christmas; she writes about friends and coworkers; and special moments others have shared with her.

Renee enjoys walking in parks, malls; creative drawing and rendering with colored markers; traveling with groups by bus, car, and checking out miscellaneous retail, rummage and garage sales. She also enjoys exercising, eating out, and light, funny movies when not writing.

When Renee was a child she wanted to get a full-time job and move out, buy her own house, get a car, get married and have a few fun children. She had dreams of becoming a dentist, artist, or perhaps start a local corner store with an ice cream counter.

Renee's poetry has also appeared in the 2015 *Encore Writers* anthology published by Grey Wolfe Publishing.

www.GreyWolfePublishing.com

Terry Sanville

Terry Sanville lives in San Luis Obispo, California with his artist-poet wife (his in-house editor) and one skittery cat (his in-house critic). He writes full time, producing short stories, essays, poems, and novels. Since 2005, his short stories have been accepted by more than 220 literary and commercial journals, magazines, and anthologies including The Potomac Review, The Bitter Oleander, Shenandoah, and Conclave: A Journal of Character. He was nominated twice for a Pushcart Prize for his stories "The Sweeper," and "The Garage." Terry is a retired urban planner and an accomplished jazz and blues guitarist – who once played with a symphony orchestra backing up jazz legend George Shearing.

Thomas K. Tabor

Tom is a retired midnight hotel desk clerk, and he managed the front desk of the YMCA Detroit for twenty-five years. Tom enjoys spending time with his brothers of the Freemasons, landscape watercolor painting, and being a life-long bachelor.

Tom wrote *The Innkeeper's Adventure* in 2016 (Grey Wolfe Publishing) to give children a fun story simply to enjoy, as he remembers his fond childhood in Augusta, Georgia.

www.GreyWolfePublishing.com

DETROIT DOG RESCUE

In 2014 Detroit Dog Rescue opened the first and only NO-KILL shelter in the city of Detroit. Since achieving that goal, they are now helping the city of Detroit become the NO-KILL city we all know it can be. DDR is helping to achieve this through: advocating for alternatives to euthanasia, proper pet care education, low cost spay and neutering programs, as well as, assisting low income families with pet food and medical resources.

Detroit Dog Rescue
P.O. Box 806119
St. Clair Shores, MI 48080

Email: detroitdogrescue@gmail.com

Phone: (313) 458-8014   Fax: (586)200-3712

Foster & adoption information line: (313) 458-8014

To report an abandoned or abused dog please call:
(313) 458-8014

www.ingramcontent.com/pod-product-compliance
Lightning Source LLC
Chambersburg PA
CBHW071939170626
46813CB00005B/1793